The Life Unlived

A novel by Jeff Pearson

This book, *The Life Unlived*, is the sequel to *Forever Across The Marsh*. It can be read as a stand-alone novel, but it's far better if you read *Forever Across The Marsh* first.

Official Website (for all books by Jeff Pearson):
www.acrossthemarsh.com

Copyright © 2024 by Jeff Pearson

All rights reserved.

This book is a work of fiction. Names, characters, businesses, organizations, places, events, and incidents either are the product of the author's imagination or are used fictitiously. Any resemblance to actual persons, living or dead, events, or locales is coincidental.

Scripture quotations contained herein are from the New Revised Standard Version Bible, copyright © 1989 by the Division of Christian Education of the National Council of the Churches of Christ in the U.S.A. and are used by permission. All rights reserved.

Amazon Paperback ISBN 978-0-9980259-3-3
Amazon Hardcover ISBN 978-0-9980259-6-4
Ingram Spark Paperback ISBN 978-0-9980259-4-0
Kindle ISBN 978-0-9980259-5-7

Official Website (for all books by Jeff Pearson):
www.acrossthemarsh.com

About the Author

Jeff Pearson is the author of *Forever Across The Marsh*, a consistent #1 Amazon Best Seller. Jeff grew up in Camden, South Carolina. A military veteran, he has served in Iraq and Afghanistan. Jeff now lives with his wife and three children in the Savannah, Georgia area, where he practices law.

As a child, Jeff had big dreams, but none included writing books. *Forever Across The Marsh* was originally intended to be a private collection of stories for his family. He thought it was an odd book full of humor that others might not appreciate. But Jeff's wife, Megan, encouraged him to publish it. It turns out that a lot of readers share Megan's opinion.

Readers of *Forever Across The Marsh* asked Jeff to write a sequel. Over the following six years, Jeff wrote several sequels, trashing them all . . . except one—*The Life Unlived*.

Here, Jeff has given you all he has to give.

In memory of Mel Pearson

*Thank you, Dad, for everything.
The world is a better place because of you.*

CHAPTER 1

A Fire Burns

Inside of everyone, a fire burns. Even when dormant, the fire keeps warm the gifts we have neglected for far too long. We all have gifts. They are the foundations of our dreams. And we all know that life is short. So why do we readily abandon our dreams as if we have more than one life to live? Why do we choose to ignore the call to do what we were put on Earth to do?

The Shadows know. They know the power of invisible forces like doubt, fear, and hate. They want us to make excuses. They want us to delay. They want us to believe that we don't matter.

My life, until a few hours ago, didn't matter. Now, I'm spending the final few hours trapped in a bell tower furiously writing these letters to you—a stranger who will probably never find them. But you deserve to know what happened. You deserve to know what we found. You deserve to know about the human code.

The Shadows understand the code. For a long time, they have used it to track us and to bend us toward their will. And, in the year that won't be mentioned, they used it to wreak havoc on our world. We weren't prepared for it. Within a few short months during that year, this became clear: the biggest threat to humans was humans.

Friends turned against friends. Family turned against family. And suddenly, those you thought you knew well seemed like strangers, distant and foreign, almost insane. Relationships that were once cherished suddenly frayed, broke, and snapped as if blown away in a storm. Millions of people died. None of us escaped unscathed.

That year, we all walked down dark roads, some darker than others. I am, right now, in the middle of my darkest hour and I don't know how it will end. Part of me clings to hope, not hope for me—as that time has passed—but hope for my family, hope for you, and hope for this small world.

The Shadows laugh at such thoughts. They live in darkness. They strive for darkness. And, in that awful year, they used all their influence and power to bring their dark world to us.

+ + +

Damn, the explosions are getting close. Mount Etna is erupting like she's never done before. And the Shadows want me dead.

CHAPTER 2

The Life Unlived

My days might be done, but you still have time to do something that matters. From what I can tell, the past hour has been the only time in my life when I had a chance to do anything that truly mattered. And all that will be lost unless some miracle keeps the Shadows away. These letters will burn with me in this bell tower and all will have been in vain.

I can't allow that to happen. Others gave too much. What they've done must matter. They heard the voice and answered its call. I must do the same.

The voice—the one I speak of—can you hear it? No? Then put these letters down for a moment and listen. Listen for a voice you once knew as a child. Listen to your soul.

The voice—the one that only you can hear—is buried beneath an emptiness that yearns to be filled. It's a voice that calls you to live your true life. The voice, it's yours. It is the voice of the life unlived.

CHAPTER 3

Near the End

The walls of this old bell tower are shaking. The floor rumbles as the explosions get even closer. Through a small opening, I can see the red glow of lava as it flows through the town square. I can feel the heat radiating from the stone walls. Even as the end approaches, I can't help but wonder, *How did we get here?* The whole world seems to have gone completely mad.

As I move away from the wall, my hand bumps against what we found on the mountain, reminding me that it was all very real. A short time ago, it seemed like a myth at best. I didn't believe Ruby. I didn't want to believe her. And, to be frank, I really didn't care. Too much had occupied my mind.

But there it is next to me, in almost perfect condition even after weathering so many centuries. And it'll burn with me in this tower, lost forever unless I can tell you what happened.

CHAPTER 4

Before the Climb

Around midnight (maybe an hour ago), we stood near the top of Mount Etna, at the start of our final climb. Have you ever seen Mount Etna? Mount Etna dominates the eastern shore of the island of Sicily. She's massive. Think Rocky Mountain high, but much broader. And violent. She's the most violent volcano in this part of the world, beautiful and frightening all at the same time. She gives life to all those that dwell on her slopes. And she takes it too. Etna has always been that way.

As I looked up toward the peak of that tall, dark mountain, thunder rolled. But I knew it wasn't thunder. Before me lay a trail disappearing into an alpine grove, the leaves trembling with fear as the ground shook around us. Dark Shadows moved about the trees while clouds of ash shielded the moon.

My friend David stood next to me with his gaze fixed on the trail before us. The winding path wove its way to the edge of the dark forest, where it disappeared.

Frozen by fear, I stared at the path before us. "We aren't going to make it, are we?"

David said nothing.

I felt anger start to rise as I looked at the impossible danger ahead of us. It wasn't supposed to end this way. This battle, this final climb, should have belonged to me and to me alone. "You can't go with me, David. You know that."

David put his hand on my shoulder and then looked at me. "Mel, you can turn back now."

A Shadow screamed ahead of us, its voice hitting us like a gust of bitter, cold wind.

"No," I said. "It's time. This must be done."

The Shadows moved quicker and grew in number. Soon, the trail would close, perhaps forever covered by hardened lava. As the tall mountain rumbled, I looked up one last time. Gritting my teeth, I took one step forward. It wasn't supposed to end this way.

CHAPTER 5

The Shadow

As I took another step up the tall, dark mountain, doubt crept in again and I froze. Paralyzing doubt stopped me in my tracks. I couldn't help but think that maybe I had been wrong all along. Nausea buckled my knees and brought me to the ground.

Then, as I fought the urge to quit, I sensed his presence. I could feel his presence. Ahead of me, a Shadow laughed, a dark, slow, deep laugh. I looked up, hoping for a glimpse of him. The Dark One had been haunting me since the frightening night across the marsh.

Clenching my fist, I cursed the Shadow. I cursed the mountain. I cursed fate. I cursed everything that had brought me there. Then, as exhaustion crept in, I felt the Shadow smile. Doubt followed with overwhelming force.

Maybe I should quit now and end it all. How did it all get to this point? I was a nobody, just another nothing man. I should have disappeared into the fog long ago. I wasn't built for this. I couldn't carry this burden.

Guilt sunk in, reminding me that this was my job. My dad would expect me to finish it. My wife Lynn would expect me to finish it. My children would be ashamed to learn that their father wasn't tough enough, that he wasn't brave enough. This was not a time to pity myself. My life might not matter, but I would climb the mountain. Hell could wait.

I took another step forward. The Shadows released a frenzy of howls. This time, I smiled. I took another step forward, backed by a confidence I hadn't felt in a long time.

"Here we go," I said aloud, taking another step up the mountain.

+ + +

As I sit here now in the bell tower writing all of this down for you, I still find it hard to believe that all of it started nearly halfway across the world, deep in a vast saltwater marsh outside a small town near Savannah, Georgia. That's where it all began.

CHAPTER 6

The Beginning

It was around Christmas, before the year that won't be mentioned. In the middle of an unusually cold Savannah night, my simple life had been turned upside down. Little did I know that the world would soon follow.

After leaving the military, I had moved to a small town outside of Savannah, Georgia, with my wife Lynn and two young children, Tyler and Sophia. I didn't have much of a plan for what my new job would be, but my father had grown up near Georgia's coast, a place he loved. The vast marsh, the saltwater rivers, and the untouched islands thrived with life. They also hid mysteries and dangers unknown. When I moved my family to the edge of that wild coast, I had no idea how it would draw me in and put me on a path to a destiny I had never imagined.

A terminal cancer diagnosis had pushed me to race across the marsh in search of riches from a sunken ship that had secretly been found. But several others, including a bully from my childhood, learned that it had been discovered. The night ended with death and heartache, but I had escaped, if only for a moment. Every bone in my body told me that the end had arrived.

Tired and still in a bit of shock, I stood outside my home looking in. While a cold darkness surrounded me, I felt warm all over as if sitting next to a crackling fire. The sweet presence of a young girl, Rosa, was with me, beside me, comforting me as a daughter might do for her father as he passes away from this world.

Through the windows, we could see my family happily dancing about our living room. Lynn and our children, Tyler and Sophia, all seemed so happy. They were oblivious to everything that had just happened.

Precious laughter filled the room as my sweet, little daughter, Sophia, led them in song:

> "Wing-a-wound the wosies.
> A pocket fuhl of posies.
> Ashes! Ashes!
> We all fwall down!"

I felt pure joy and pain all at the same time. Oh, how I wanted to be part of it once again!

As if she heard my thoughts, Rosa squeezed my hand and said, "Not everyone gets a second chance."

I knelt eye-level to Rosa and peered into her eyes. Mine filled with tears, but she smiled and said, "Some of us never get a first."

Her sweet voice warmed my soul. Radiating with gentle confidence, she turned and looked at my family. "Go," she said. "Go be with them."

More than anything, I wanted to go. I wanted to be with my family. But Rosa's presence had changed something inside of me. I couldn't leave her. Part of me wanted to join her. I felt drawn to her, and at the same time, drawn to Lynn, Sophia, and Tyler. It was as if I were paralyzed, unable to choose between the living and the dead. I felt I had one foot in our world and one foot in another.

She released my hand and nudged me toward my living room. "Go. It's not your time."

Time, I thought. Time had been racing by, but now it seemed to stand still. *Time*, I wondered, *how much time did I have?*

Again, as if reading my mind, Rosa said, "I don't know. None of us do."

Rosa smiled and then motioned behind her. There were other Spirits standing together against the night's edge. Two Spirits stepped forward and came into focus. My grandparents stood before me in almost living color. They looked so lovely and happy together, as if all their worries had been washed away. They looked at me as if I had simply been away for too long. I felt the urge to run and hug them both, so much so that I rose to my feet and began to walk toward them. But Rosa, with her gentle touch, pulled me back.

"Not yet," she said. "You can't join us now. There is work left undone."

I peered at the host of others standing behind my grandparents. I knew them, most of them, if not all. There were childhood friends that had passed too soon. Distant relatives. There were others I knew by face, but I had forgotten their names. The desire to join them almost overwhelmed me.

Sensing this, Rosa said again, "Not now."

Confused, I looked at Rosa, wondering why.

"You have been called," she said.

"Called?"

"Yes," she said, now almost in a whisper. "It's not something we can talk about here."

A sudden chill ran down my back. The cold reality of the night came racing back like a gust of wind.

Rosa looked around, searching for someone else who might be watching. She leaned towards me. "The Shadows are coming. They might be listening now. Go. Be with your family. And listen to Ruby."

Ruby? I thought. Ruby was a witch-like woman that I barely knew. She could be found on River Street in Savannah at times, providing "readings" to people about their future. My neighbor David had introduced me to Ruby after I told him about Rosa's spirit visiting me.

"Yes," Rosa said in her young, sweet voice. "You must learn to trust Ruby. She is a link to us, to those that others can't see."

I began to speak, but Rosa touched her finger to her lips. "I must go now. They're almost here."

Rosa moved toward the other Spirits.

"Will I see you again?" I asked.

She turned and smiled. "When it's time. Now go."

Off in the distance, I heard a hideous laugh. My grandparents and the group of Spirits moved quickly. Rosa followed, looking back one last time before vanishing into the night.

+ + +

With the Spirits gone, I stood alone in my backyard. It was then when reality began to come into view. Cancer riddled my body. I could feel its weight again. Still in shock from the night's events, I wondered how I could explain it all to Lynn and our children. They needed to know. They deserved to know.

But how does a father tell his children that he's dying? It would spoil their happiness, and for what? And what if Rosa was right? What if I had been given a second chance?

I didn't know what to do. I couldn't see wrong from right or best from worst. All of it seemed muddled together.

I couldn't tell my children yet. They wouldn't understand. Lynn must know, but that could wait one more night. Perhaps a good night's sleep would bring clarity. As I wrung my hands with indecision, a blast of cool air blew shivers down my back again and the warm house called me in. I felt the urge to go inside and be with my family.

In moments like these, when a person nears the end, life comes to a well-defined point. And every life is different. Mine, in sum, had been one disaster after another. Chaos was my home. I, Melvin Scott, tried to do too much, too fast, with little concern for how it might end. But oh, it had made for some great times. Even the chaos seemed to comfort me. Family and chaos went hand in hand.

My family seemed so happy. I would miss them. I wanted to hug my children and tell them how much I loved them. I would give anything for more time with my children. If only I could bottle up their laughter and take it with me, wherever I was headed next. That would get me through the dark times. Overcome with the desire to stay in this world, I fell to my knees and wept.

It was at that very moment when I felt the Shadow. The hair on the back of my neck stood straight. Someone, something was watching me. Suddenly full of adrenaline and alert, I turned to face him. But, just as the Shadow had made his presence known, he vanished into the night. Yet he was still there, off in the distance, barely blending in with the darkness.

I had felt that way several times before. Once on the bluff, right before I saw my childhood nemesis Judd Nero on Charcoal's treasure-hunting boat. And another time, only a few hours earlier, on Jesse's Island.

I scanned the night, looking for any sign of the Shadow. I knew he stood nearby. As my adrenaline peaked and my senses sharpened, I saw two green eyes begin to glow. No longer fearing Nero, I took one step toward the Shadow. The green eyes narrowed and the Shadow began to laugh. As his voice rose, a dark and powerful force overwhelmed me. I tried to take another step forward, but my knees buckled. The force hit stronger than any before. Exhaustion took over. Tunnel-vision closed in, squeezing out all light. The Shadow laughed again and I collapsed on the ground.

CHAPTER 7

An Awakening

Have you ever had a near-death experience? I'm not talking about a close call on the highway; I'm talking about an out-of-body, I-thought-I-was-dead experience. Time—if such a concept exists in that moment—slows down to a halt. The past, present, and future become all muddled into one. And if you're lucky, you feel completely at peace. Then you wake up. That's the whole point of a near-death experience. You didn't actually die; you just got very near to it.

After one's awakening, life looks very different than it did before. At first, you treat every second as if it's your last. You treasure your time with those you love. Time is now a gift. You focus on those you love most, while the rest of the world around you fades away. You dance. You smile. You laugh. You hug as if it's the very last time. It is as if heaven has arrived here on Earth.

Then, as time passes, you forget about the gift of time and your view of the world begins to change. You notice things that before might have passed you by. Selfishness, greed, suffering, and injustice abound. The world spins under a dark cloud and you wonder, *What is it all about? Why even try?* You lose ambition. You withdraw from society, seeing it all as absurd. Relationships wither. Hope all but dies. You live only for the sake of a precious few. Yet, unless they too have traveled down the same dark road, even the precious few don't understand the burden you carry.

If you've ever lived on the edge of death, then you know that dreams feel like a different experience. Of course, we're all dying. But when you know death is coming for you soon, dreams become something more. It's as if you're straddling two worlds. Dreams intertwine with what we think is real. Dreams draw the past and the future closer together. In our dreams, we see those we once knew and meet others we've not yet known. No longer encumbered by traditional notions of what we've accepted as real and true, dreams become places where we can walk and talk with others, searching for answers, meaning, and purpose.

In my first dream after that night across the marsh, I found myself meandering about the times and places of the past and of the future. I saw my grandparents, Nana and Grandaddy, who had appeared during Rosa's visit. This time, Nana and Grandaddy were at their farm in Georgia. They walked together around the property in no particular hurry. They tended to the chickens and moved about the yard, steadily going about a day's work. As I stood watching, they waved with a casual pleasantness. It was like our encounter was just another warm, summer day. In that comforting dream, I knew I would someday see them again.

I wanted to spend the entire dream resting under a shade tree on the farm. But the dream shifted. As quickly as the old farm appeared, it vanished, and I found myself on the slopes of Mount Etna, looking up toward her towering, smoldering peak. Thunder rolled, but I knew it wasn't thunder. Etna was awakening from a long slumber. As I stood in awe of the smoke billowing from her giant crater, a sharp wind blew across my back. Leaves on the trees around me trembled. Etna roared and lava erupted from her crater. In a flash, I found myself back in the small town I once called home.

I grew up in Sandy Pines, a rural area just outside the city limits of Camden, South Carolina. It's a wonderful place and all I knew as a child. In my dream, I was an eight-year-old kid again, playing with my friends. Together, we explored the neighborhood woods, which seemed like a wilderness back then.

We quickly moved from the woods to an overgrown field, throwing a ball back and forth. Easily transitioning from one game and place to another, we moved to a dusty dirt road, riding our bikes without a care in the world. No traffic. No helmets. Just a bunch of kids on an old dirt road. One friend took his hands off the handlebars and sped away. Another popped a wheelie and raced after the first boy. At some point, they both crashed and fell into a ditch. The rest of us stopped and rolled off our bikes, laughing and goofing off as children do. It was a wonderful time. I tried to savor the laughter. It was like music for the soul. Among the laughter of the past, I could hear the laughter of others. At first, it was all muddled together. Then I realized that the laughter was the laughter of my own children, Tyler and Sophia. It was laughter not of the past or future, but of the present.

Their laughter slowly woke me from my slumber and the dreams began to fade. I soon found myself in our bedroom again, half-awake in our home near the marsh. Even half-asleep, I sensed that the laughter was coming from our living room. My eyes opened wide and the dreams disappeared. It *was* coming from my living room. There were other noises, a commotion in the kitchen and a crowd of voices. I heard my father, my mother, my wife Lynn, and even my brother-in-law Danny. *Odd*, I thought. Then I heard David's voice and Ruby's too. *This can't be real*, I thought. But I could smell bacon sizzling on the stove. An aroma of warm coffee filled the air. Someone dropped something on the floor, and I suddenly sat up, bumping against the headboard. For a moment, all the noises stopped. Then footsteps raced toward my room.

Sitting up in bed, I realized that I had not died. The confusion I heard in my kitchen could neither be heaven nor hell. The confusion was, in every way, life. Real life.

Who knows how long I had been out. Long enough to draw an unusual crowd. More than anything, I wanted to see my family. I felt the urge to hug them as they raced toward me. I wanted to tell them how much I loved them.

The first figure rounded a corner in my room and stood at the foot of my bed. It would be my first human contact since nearly going to the other side. My encounters with the supernatural had taken a toll. Something inside of me yearned for human contact. An unusual burst of emotion thickened my throat. I could barely wait to hug and hold the first person who reached me.

Then he appeared. It was Danny. "Hey, man," he said. "You finally done with your little nap?"

Dammit, I thought. Even when I was near death, my brother-in-law's presence annoyed me. "Hello, Danny."

This, I knew, was real life. Real, unfiltered life.

After taking a sip from his coffee (at least I thought it was coffee), Danny burped. "Dang. That one burned my nose hairs."

Lynn appeared, gently nudged Danny aside, and looked at me. "How do you feel?"

"Ok, I guess." I rubbed the back of my head. "My head's still in a fog."

Danny took another sip of his drink. "Probably bumped it when you passed out in the yard. Either that or it's a hangover."

I didn't even bother to respond. Behind Lynn, a series of heads peered around the corner. Lynn walked over to me and put her hand on my shoulder. "You've been asleep for over 24 hours."

Confused, I said. "Why is everyone here?"

Danny laughed. "I told you he didn't know. I tried to tell him when he came over to my house. But he was talking all crazy like and walking around in a fog."

"Tell me what?" I asked.

"See? He doesn't get it. As usual, he's oblivious to it all," Danny said, this time with an unusual hint of actual concern. "The whole-damned world is collapsing, and he deals with it by going out all night and getting drunk. What were you thinking, Mel? This ain't college."

I had known Danny my entire life and had never sensed that he was concerned about anything. Long before he married my sister, Danny had grown up with me in the same small town. We had been through times that I thought were the worst, and he had always navigated through it with such ease and calmness that I didn't believe he cared about anything. Danny's unusual tone left me even more confused.

Danny walked closer to where I was resting. "I'm sorry, Mel. We'll get through this. I just don't like it. I don't like where it's going."

Where "what" is going? Did he know about the night across the marsh?

In an unusual display of affection, he put his hand on my shoulder. Then he turned around and left. Lynn leaned toward me and kissed my forehead. "I know you weren't drinking that night. We can talk about it later. There's a lot going on right now."

Did she know about that night? She must know, but how?

When Lynn walked out of the room, David entered. David was an interesting guy, my neighbor and pastor of a local church who had gone through his own soul searching. David had been with me during the night across the marsh and looked at me with eyes full of energy and excitement. He whispered, "You're going to be fine, Mel. There's so much we need to talk about."

I leaned toward David, looking behind him to make sure no others could hear, and asked, "Do they know?"

He shook his head. "No." His eyes showed no concern. "It's so exciting. And we need to act quickly. There was something else on that old shipwreck. Something more valuable than any amount of gold or silver."

I squinted my eyes, still lost in confusion.

David continued, "We'll talk later this afternoon. You, me, and Ruby. I've got it all planned out."

"Ruby?" I asked.

"Yes, she's here," David said. "We're all here."

Finally, I mustered up the energy to get out of bed and stumbled toward all the noise. In the hallway, I met my father and mother. David, still full of excitement, waved and then left us alone.

Dad seemed calm and steady, but I could feel his anxiety. Mom held his arm. I was almost forty years old, but still their child. I felt unexpected emotions well up in my eyes as I hugged Mom. My throat thickened again, preventing speech.

Dad stepped back and folded his arms. "Well, Son, how's the hangover?"

Mom pinched his side.

My throat cleared. "Dad, I wasn't out drinking. I..."

"I know, Son. So does your mother. We are your parents."

"Did David talk to you?"

"David?" Dad responded. "No. Look. Whatever happened the other night is your business. You can tell me when you're ready. Or not. Just know that we're here for you, Son. Always."

Mom wiped tears from her eyes and tried to compose herself. "I'm sorry, Mel. There's just so much going on right now. And I'm so glad you're back with us."

Dad put his arm around Mom. "Let's go, honey. He's alright now. We've got to get back to Camden before the roads close."

What? Why would the roads close?

As my parents walked away, Tyler and Sophia came bounding down the stairs and hugged me.

"Daddy!" Sophia exclaimed. "You've been fweepin fwor a wong time."

"Yeah, Dad," Tyler said. "Mommy never lets us sleep that late."

I stretched my arms toward both of them. "Come here!"

They jumped into my arms, and I squeezed them as if I hadn't seen them for years. It was like coming home from a long military deployment. There's no feeling like holding those you love after being gone for far too long.

Sophia wiggled out of my embrace, leaned back, and said, "Daddy?"

"Yes, Sweetie?"

"You stink," she said.

Tyler sniffed. "Yeah, Dad. You smell like fish, like low tide on the marsh."

So much for the embrace. I took one whiff of the air and regained my senses. Something smelled awful. Terribly awful, worse than a wet dog. That something was me.

"Y'all give Daddy a few minutes to clean up, ok?"

Sophia looked at Tyler. "I fink he smwells whike poop."

Tyler grinned. "Poop," he said. Sophia giggled.

"Poop."

"Poop. Poop. Poop."

"Enough!" I said, getting my dad-voice back again. "No more of this talk about poop."

Sophia laughed. "Daddy said poop!"

"Get out of here!"

Of all the things. Life again, unfiltered. I was back.

+ + +

Few things in this world have more healing power than a hot shower. Mine was oh so wonderful. It was like washing the past few days away. But when I finished, I still couldn't shake a single, burning question.

What in the hell was going on?

Now, if you lived through the year that won't be mentioned, then you know how, almost overnight, the world turned completely upside down.

What year is it for you right now? In what year did you find these letters? It matters because the world, in the year that won't be mentioned, was experiencing transformational changes.

A plague—a virus—took a dark, firm grip on our lives. But there were other things, other invisible forces, that were reshaping and wreaking havoc on humans.

Technology raced forward at a stunning speed. But most of us didn't know what was happening behind the scenes. We didn't know how deeply it was terrorizing us. The Internet had been around for years, allowing humans—good and bad—to connect instantly. This produced fertile ground for what was to come.

Smartphones had put the Internet (and a powerful computer) in the hands of almost everyone. But it was social media that brought the real tipping point. Social media became the king, queen, and absolute ruler of influence. It dominated the human mind. It was social media that gave tremendous power to those who knew how to use it.

Even those who rejected social media were under its influence. They just didn't realize it. The data gathered by smartphones allowed small groups of people—those with financial means and technological know-how—to influence others with unprecedented precision and accuracy.

Our smartphones showed us ads of things we wanted, seemingly right before or exactly during the moments when we wanted those things. It was as if our phones were reading our minds. Here's what was actually happening: the smartphones were collecting enormous troves of data on the things we did—what we bought, what we searched for, what we read, what we watched, where we traveled, and countless other habits and patterns. Smartphones sent this information to servers, which learned our tendencies, habits, and desires at an exponential rate.

Companies quickly embraced social media as their primary way to advertise their products. But it was in the field of politics, where smartphones, data, and social media created the most dangerous perils.

Elections could be bought and sold. People with means and technological savviness could distribute propaganda with frightening precision and effectiveness. Foreign nations and foreign actors–both friends and foes–could blast a neighborhood with propaganda, misinformation, and sometimes even facts. Small communities in swing states became common targets. Nothing in our history had prepared us for this.

Never before had our world experienced the convergence of these powers. Still, the most frightening technology had yet to fully emerge.

Artificial intelligence existed, but it was operating behind the scenes, learning our ways and improving its effectiveness. During that dark year, AI was still generally under the control of humans. In other words, someone had to program AI to act a certain way. Humans could tell AI whether to promote messages of love and hope or spread messages of hate and fear. Humans could code AI to allow for free speech or to censor dissent. AI governed most of what we saw.

I ask you now: which message—fear or hope—carries more power? Which message carries more influence? Which message is more likely to impact your decisions? Now, think about all the people around you. Which message has more influence on them?

That year, dark forces reveled in all that was happening. They delighted in the growing effectiveness of their invisible powers.

To you who find these letters, I ask: Do you believe in invisible forces? Do you believe in the constant battle between good and evil? Do you believe that there are powers greater than you and me?

If you don't believe in invisible forces, then I wonder why you are still reading these letters. Or perhaps that is exactly why you are still with me. Perhaps you have an open mind and are curious as to why people engage in irrational, illogical, and self-destructive behavior. Perhaps you think that there might be some power more intelligent than us.

For whatever it's worth, I don't believe that humans are the most intelligent forces (for lack of a better word) in the natural and supernatural world. We—every single one of us—are clumsy creatures. And unlike AI, we often cede reason to emotion. Compared to AI, the human brain is an infant child. We don't understand ourselves, much less those around us. Luck and fate, not logic, govern our destiny.

Yes, the human experience is a very clumsy experience. That is the life I've known. It has been a good one too. Way too short, of course, but a wonderful life, full of wonderful people whom I will dearly miss. Oh, how often we take for granted the special bonds with those we've loved. Far too often we walk a path that leads to loneliness.

But enough of that. The Shadows want me to quit. And they want you to quit too. They don't want you to know what they know. They don't want you to know what happened.

Now, let's get back to my home by the marsh, during the morning I awoke from a deep sleep. I had just finished taking a hot shower. The smell of bacon and warm coffee hit my nose. Busy voices bustled about the kitchen and the living room. And I still had no idea what was going on.

+ + +

One good thing about chaos is you can get lost in it. You can almost hide in it. In chaos, your problems can vanish from the eyes of others who simply have too much going on to care about you.

In that awful year, the world turned to chaos almost overnight, but as far as I could see, it had little, if anything, to do with the night across the marsh.

After drying off with a warm towel, I found a pair of comfortable clothes and made my way to the sweet smells of our kitchen.

Isn't it nice how, in our most trying times, we can find joy in the simplest of things? Ordinary experiences like sitting down to a plate of bacon, eggs, and cheese over a soft biscuit. I sipped a cup of dark, black coffee and closed my eyes to absorb the noise of my family around me.

Does it get any better than that?

Perhaps. But not much.

The adults milled about, still talking about shutdowns, roadblocks, and things that didn't make sense. They largely ignored me, allowing me to eat my breakfast in peace. It was David who first found a seat beside me.

"How do you feel?" he asked.

"Ok," I said.

"Great," David said. "We need to talk. When you finish eating, can we…"

Danny sat down on the other side of me. "What's going on, Rip Van Winkle?"

Rather than engage with Danny, I focused on my biscuit.

Danny looked toward our living room and nodded his head toward a woman sitting in a chair by a window. In the chair—my favorite chair—Ruby sat quietly. Her presence, clearly odd and out of place, didn't disturb the others.

David knew her well, but he was alone in that regard. I can only describe Ruby as a witch. A bona fide, real-life, able-to-talk-to-dead-people witch. And she looked like a witch in every way you think a witch would look. Even though I barely knew her, she seemed to know more about me than I knew myself. I didn't trust her, yet there she sat in my living room as my children played on the floor in front of her.

Danny turned to David. "Hey, man, I think your lady friend wants you." As Ruby nodded and David walked over to her, I thought, *This situation can't get any weirder.*

Danny, scrolling on his phone, leaned toward me. "Listen to this, man. A guy just broke the record for cannonball run."

"Cannonball run?" I asked.

"Yeah, man, this dude drove from New York to LA in about 26 hours. For years, people have tried to break the record. Scientists have calculated the perfect number of stops for fuel. The perfect time of day to try. The perfect speed. The perfect times to avoid cops and miss traffic. It's a real science, man. And this dude filled his trunk and backseat with gas tanks and drove hell's bells all the way to LA."

Danny took another sip of his drink and then continued. "No science. No calculators. Just pure badass. Dude's my hero."

I looked at Danny, then at Ruby, then at David, and then at my family. It was all so jumbled. I thought, *Maybe I did die, and this is some strange version of purgatory.* I couldn't make sense of any of it. I had been so focused on my own issues that I woke up to this new wild world with no warning or explanation. To get some clarity, I leaned toward Danny and said quietly, "Danny, tell me what's no-kidding going on right now. Shoot me straight. I don't need any more of this cannonball-run nonsense."

"Sure, Mel." Danny put his drink down and said, in a no-nonsense tone, "A man ate a bat from a wet market in China. Now, millions of people are going to die."

I squeezed my fist, scrunched my eyes, and vented, "Danny, I can't take any more of this bullshit. It's not funny."

Danny didn't laugh. "C'mon, man. Let's get some fresh air."

Danny's tone told me that he wasn't messing with me. He believed what he said. He walked toward the door and I followed. As we left, David almost sprung from his chair.

Outside, I saw something I hadn't seen in a long time—Danny's truck. A beat-up, jacked-up, two-seater pickup truck. It was a rattling death trap and the most impractical piece of machinery on the road.

"Beautiful, ain't she?" Danny said.

I felt myself nodding, my mind suddenly full of memories of the many miles we'd put on Danny's truck, most of them from rides to nowhere on an empty tank of gas.

"I've kept her garaged for almost twenty years. Didn't know why," Danny said. "I couldn't sell her for a song."

"And she still runs?" I asked.

"She made it here," Danny said. "C'mon."

As I walked toward Danny's old truck, a hand touched my shoulder. I turned. "Oh. Hey, David."

"Do you have a minute?" David asked. "We need to talk."

Danny stepped toward us. "Nope. Mel's going with me."

"It won't take long. Just a few minutes," David said.

"No, sir," Danny said. "I know how that works. One minute turns into another minute. Then Mel gets distracted by something. That's another ten to thirty minutes. Then someone else comes along. Look, we'll be back soon."

"Just a few seconds," David said.

Danny was right. He knew how a sequence of events could suck someone into a never-ending vortex of distractions. Naturally, Danny never got caught up in such things, but I was a magnet for them.

I turned to Danny and said, "Just a few minutes, Danny."

He didn't say anything. He walked straight to his truck and fired the ignition. Blue and white smoke billowed from the exhaust. Something exploded. The hood shook and shivered as the pitiful, old engine roared to life. Danny walked over to the passenger side and opened the door. Then he took my arm and escorted me to the truck. As I'd done a thousand times before, I put one foot on the step rail and jumped up to the bucket seat. As Danny slammed the door, I heard a piece of metal clang against the ground. I rolled the window down to say something to David, but the window got stuck. The door was jammed, so I didn't mess with it. Danny got into the driver's seat, looked back, shifted in reverse, and roared down the driveway backwards.

I yelled through the window toward David, who looked a bit stunned. "We'll talk when I get back!"

And like that, we were off.

+ + +

In a stunningly short amount of time, Danny had made millions. How? Doing what he did best—nothing. While the rest of the world slaved away, Danny had mastered the art of making commissions off things other people sold. Luck followed him wherever he went. After a few short years of making millions, he retired (from what, I'm still not sure) and became an investor. I knew no others who enjoyed such a run of financial success. But none of this changed Danny. He was still Danny.

Despite his wealth, or perhaps because of it, Danny had kept his old truck. It seemed to be in the same condition as it was when we were seventeen.

As we rolled down the road, I asked, "Where are we going?"

"Nowhere," Danny replied.

I nodded. That was about the only thing I had heard all day that made sense. Danny and I had traveled thousands of miles on the way to nowhere. That's what we did when we were young and free of responsibility.

At first, we just rode, with the truck rumbling down the road as the only sound. Danny's truck shook and rattled just as it had done more than twenty years before. On the smooth patches of road, I sipped my coffee. The sun rose over the edge of trees passing by, warming the side of my face. As if drugged, my head bobbed in and out of a light stupor.

For a while, Danny said nothing and I fought off sleep. Then he broke the silence. "So, you really don't know what's going on?"

"No," I said.

"It's wild, man. It's crazy. The whole world is about to go bat-shit-crazy," Danny said. "I think this is going to mess people up. I'm already getting the jitters."

"What do you mean?" I asked.

With one hand on the wheel, Danny looked at me. "Think about it, Mel. The government is telling everyone to stay in their homes and, if they go outside, to keep their distance from people. Did you hear that? They're telling humans to stay away from humans."

"Doesn't sound so bad," I said.

"It ain't human, man! That's not how we work. It's not how some of us work."

I thought about the idea of taking a break from everything and found some relief in it. But Danny was all shaken up. He asked, "You know what's one of my biggest fears?"

"Responsibility?"

"No. Getting trapped on a deserted island somewhere far off in the ocean."

"Danny, some people spend a lot of money to do that. It's called vacation."

"Well, it's not for me. Scariest movie I've ever seen in my life was *Castaway*."

"What about *Lord of the Flies*?"

"No," Danny said. "They weren't alone in *Lord of the Flies*. They had each other. So long as they had that, they had hope."

"I don't think that was the point of the movie," I said.

"Doesn't matter," Danny said. "The government is a bunch of fools if they think they can keep people cooped up. It won't last two weeks. Around here, it won't last two days."

Danny drove on. I tried to comprehend what he was saying, but there were too many missing pieces. I took a sip of my coffee and then turned to Danny. "Is it really that bad? I mean, what are the experts predicting?"

"Experts. Psh," Danny said. "There ain't a human on this planet that is an expert on this. But they've got numbers. You're a numbers guy. So listen to this. A few weeks ago, a guy in China caught this virus. He walks into a room, and the virus starts doubling. Then those people passed it on to others. Almost half of them don't know they have it. So, they gave it to someone else. Nobody knows how many people it will kill. Some say 97% will survive. But that means 3% won't. Over 300 million people in the United States. Do that math?"

"Damn," I said.

"Yeah. Damn. And it's already here. It hit New York. And it's only a matter of time before it spreads."

We rode on. The road passed through an old pine forest and then opened to an overpass.

Danny pointed. "Look, the Interstate. Want to head to Camden? Ride down some dirt roads like the good ole days?"

Danny started to speed up.

"Didn't you say there were checkpoints?"

The onramp came into view. Danny looked at me and grinned. "Cannonball run!"

He floored it, and his old truck tried to roar into high gear, which, of course, it didn't have. As the large mud tires violently beat against the road, I grabbed the oh-shit bar above the window. Right before we reached the onramp, Danny's phone rang.

He slowed the truck to a reasonable speed and answered the call. "Hello?"

Danny's look changed. A few seconds later he put the phone down and turned the wheel hard, launching the truck into a near spin. Before I could respond, we were heading back home. Finally, I let go of the handlebar. "Who was that?"

Danny looked straight ahead, steadily increasing speed. "It was your mom. Your dad fell. She thinks he had a stroke."

CHAPTER 8

The Stroke

We made it back to my house in record time. Before Danny's truck fully stopped, I jumped out, ran to my porch, and burst through the front door. I found everyone—except Tyler and Sophia—sitting in our living room. Dr. Manning, who had become a friend of mine, had arrived and was tending to Dad.

"What happened?" I asked.

David approached me and said, "Mel, your dad was taking a walk with me outside. He was doing just fine. There were no warning signs. We even prayed together. Then, he suddenly fell to the ground. His arm went limp and flailed uncontrollably. His face cringed, and I could tell he was in pain. It lasted nearly a minute, and then it passed. He's doing better now."

I heard Dad's voice from the couch. "I'm doing fine," Dad said. "You're all overreacting."

Dr. Manning paused his examination of Dad and said, "He's not showing any cognitive impact at the moment. I'm quite surprised. I would have expected a more lasting impact, but strokes do odd things."

I walked over and asked, "How do you feel, Dad?"

"I'm fine, Son," he said. "Don't worry about me. These things happen."

"Yes," Dr. Manning said. "They do happen, but it's a serious matter. You should get to your doctor and have an MRI immediately."

"I will. I will," Dad said. "We were getting our things together to go back to Camden before all of this happened."

Dad looked at Mom and said, "Honey, are you ready?"

"I think you should get an MRI here, right now," Mom said.

Dad shook his head. "No. There's no need for that. We can be in Camden in a few hours. We'll take care of it there. Now that Mel's back, let's go."

"But Dad," I said. "You're welcome to stay here. I think Mom's right."

"No, I'm going home and that's final," he said.

We all knew he meant it too. When Dad wanted to go somewhere, that was it. Everyone got up and did what they could to help Mom and Dad, getting the rest of their bags and packing some food.

I went over to Dad to help him to the car. When I reached for his arm, he said, "I'm fine, Son. Really."

And from most accounts, he was. At least, it seemed that way. As we were walking to his car, he found a moment when we were out of earshot of the others. Dad turned to me and said, "Son, I don't know what's going on. But I know something's bothering you. And it's not my little stroke."

"I'm doing ok, Dad," I said.

"Maybe," he said. "But maybe not. Either way, that's your business. But you know that if you need anything, if you need any help, I'm here for you. No questions."

"Dad," I said. "You're the one who just had a stroke."

"Yeah, well," he said, "we're going to get this thing figured out and deal with it."

We walked to his car, where Mom was waiting. Wasting no time, Dad got in, buckled his seatbelt, and waved goodbye. And like that, they were off.

That was Dad. That's who he was. And who were we to hold him back? Dad had undoubtedly battled more than his share of illnesses. He'd already fought and beaten several forms of cancer. He had faced difficult odds before and prevailed. I don't wish physical suffering on anyone. But good does come from those experiences. They harden one's grit, building a toughness that can repel forces like fear and worry. Men like Dad don't scatter.

After Dad left, David approached me again and said, "Your father really is a wonderful man."

"Yes, he is," I said, almost to myself. Then I asked David, "What were you and Dad talking about? That is, right before the stroke."

"Mel, sometimes people confide in me with the expectation that I will keep those conversations private," David said.

I nodded. "I understand," I said. "It's just not like Dad to pray with people he doesn't know that well."

"Mel, you trust me, don't you?"

"Yes," I said.

"That was enough for him," David said. "I know this is a difficult and odd time for you, but we need to talk. You, me, and Ruby. As soon as possible."

"No," I said. "David, I'm exhausted. And no offense, but I'd like some time away from Ruby. I'd like some time away from everyone. I need to spend time with my family."

David sighed. "I understand, but it's very important that you speak with Ruby. There was much more than gold on that ship they found. It's so old and so valuable that I'm uncomfortable speaking of it even here."

"I don't care how much it's worth," I said. "I don't need it now."

"It has nothing to do with money," David said. "Will you do one thing for me? Just one. And if you decide to walk away, then I won't mention it again. I'll leave you alone."

"What is it?" I asked.

"Spend an hour listening to Ruby," David said. "One hour tomorrow morning at my church."

I took a deep breath. "Then she'll leave me alone, too?"

"Yes," David said. "If you so choose."

"Ok," I said. "One hour. Tomorrow."

David's eyes lit up with excitement. "Thank you, Mel."

"One hour," I repeated. "And then I'm done."

"Ok, I'll tell her," David said, almost racing to his car.

As David left, Dr. Manning approached me and said, "Mel, how do *you* feel?"

"I'm doing ok."

"Have you told your family about your cancer yet?" Dr. Manning asked.

"No. Only David knows."

"Denial is a common response for people in your condition," Dr. Manning said. "But you'll need to tell your family at some point. Especially Lynn. They deserve to know."

"Yes," I said. "But here's the thing, Doc. I actually feel ok right now. I feel better today than when you gave me the news. Isn't there a chance I can beat it? Could your scans have been wrong? At least, to some degree?"

"Very unlikely, Mel," Dr. Manning said. "There is little that medicine can do for you now." Dr. Manning paused, appearing to reflect upon my condition. "Mel, do you believe in miracles?"

"I don't know."

"It's not my job to get hopes up, Mel," Dr. Manning said. "As a doctor, I rely on data and patterns to make objective decisions. Those things lead me to conclude that your time here is limited. As a friend, I can tell you that some things happen that I can't explain. In my field, we call them outliers. We don't count on them. If you were to beat this disease, then you would be an outlier. It's not something you should count on, Mel. Go be with your family."

"I understand," I said. "And thank you. For everything."

I was going to ask him to send me the bill for Dad. I'd let him know that I could pay for it, which was now true. But I stopped short, which was unlike me. Somehow, I knew he wouldn't accept it. Some people are that way.

CHAPTER 9

The Keepers Codex

Early the next morning, I heard a knock on our front door. Still exhausted, I eased from my bed and pulled on some jeans. Except for my footsteps, all was quiet. I opened the front door and was immediately met with David's excited voice. "Good morning!" he said. "I have warm coffee in my car. C'mon, let's go to the church before people begin to wake. Ruby's there waiting for us."

Rubbing my eyes, I responded, "What? Oh, yeah. Can we do this a little later?"

David grabbed my arm. "C'mon. Let's go. We'll get you back here soon, I promise."

Before I could resist, David had shuffled me into the car.

Not yet out of my driveway, David said, "I can barely believe it! I have to pinch my arm to remind myself this is all happening!"

As his car rolled along the road, I leaned my head against the window and tried to doze off. In a few minutes, I found myself dozing in and out of a comfortable sleep. Meanwhile, David carried on as if I were listening.

On the way to David's church, I slowly began to wake up, the ride now pleasantly quiet. In an almost involuntary way, my hand found a cup of warm coffee. With my eyes closed, I leaned back against the seat and sipped the coffee, easing into the day as the pine trees and oaks dripping with moss sped along my window.

It was all very peaceful until David broke the silence. "There is so much to tell you, Mel. I'm still learning myself. Ruby was right. She has so much to tell you."

My eyes still closed, I nodded, perhaps involuntarily or perhaps to not be rude. The reality was that I didn't care. I entirely and sincerely didn't care. Looking back on it now, from this bell tower, I realize that the ride to David's church was the first time I was introduced to the human code—an invisible code that governs our behavior. David was trying, whether he knew it or not, to show me one of the fundamental elements of that code. For most of the drive, David was excited, like someone who had learned of a transformational idea and couldn't help but share that discovery with a friend. David believed in what he said.

As we neared the church, David grew serious. "It's not all good. Some of it is quite dark. Mel, are you familiar with cognitive dissonance?"

I barely opened my eyes, let out a lion-like yawn, and turned to David. "Sorry, David. Do I know who?"

"Not who," David said. "Cognitive dissonance. It's a way of saying that your mind and body experience stress when you learn facts that are inconsistent with your beliefs. Then, you rearrange the facts to be consistent with your own beliefs."

I responded, "English, please."

"Let's see," David said. "If you're offended, you stop listening. You tune out whatever is said next. If you're confused, you stop listening. You make sense of whatever is happening based on your own personal beliefs."

I shifted in my seat. "Ok. And?"

"It's important, Mel. It's like poison. For some of us, it's worse than poison. Mel, people like me hold strong beliefs. Our beliefs and values guide us. Our beliefs drive our decisions and give us purpose and meaning. When people like me hear facts that challenge our beliefs, we deny or reject those facts. If we can't deny the facts, then our minds naturally try to rearrange the facts in a way that's more consistent with our beliefs."

David paused as if expecting a response.

I thought to myself, "Well, that sounds dumb."

David tensed up, clearly offended.

"Did I say that out loud?" I asked. "I'm sorry. What I meant to say was that... how do I say this politely? David, I hear what you're saying. I'm listening. But here's the thing. I really don't care."

David looked straight ahead, silent. He seemed to be holding his breath, almost in anger.

Finally, David exhaled. "Can't you see, Mel? It still has a firm grip on me. Cognitive dissonance is real."

I nodded.

He continued, "And you can't call people dumb."

"I didn't mean to say that. And I wasn't calling *you* dumb. I was talking about the idea of rearranging facts to fit one's beliefs. It just seemed..."

"Mel, stop. People don't like to be wrong. Cognitive dissonance *is* a big deal," David said, almost slamming the brakes. "It might not mean much to you, Mel. But it ruins lives."

David's car pulled into the church parking lot. He parked the car and looked directly at me. "Mel, remember the time when I wasn't acting like myself?"

"Are you talking about the months when you wore sackcloth and wandered around mumbling incoherently?"

"Yes," David said. "I never told you why. It happened at Easter, during one of my church services. I had prepared a powerful message for the congregation. A message about trusting the Bible and believing that every word is true. I believed this with all my heart. It's why I became a Rabbi and why I later became a Minister. I believed in both the Old Testament and The New with all my soul. That Easter morning, I had prepared a powerful message based on the death and resurrection of Yeshua."

"Who?" I asked.

"Yeshua," David said. "I don't call him by his other name. Not anymore. His other name, more so than any other, invokes bias. His name triggers cognitive dissonance like no other."

"Ok," I said.

"In preparation for that sermon, I studied the Book of John. According to John, Yeshua was the sacrificial lamb crucified on Passover, before the Passover meal." David explained. "But there was a problem."

David paused and seemed to well up with tears. Something still had a hold of him.

"So, what was the problem?"

"Yeshua could not have been crucified before the Passover meal, not according to the other Gospels. The Last Supper—the meal Yeshua had with his disciples before crucifixion—was the Passover meal! The Book of John got it wrong," David said, looking directly at me.

I paused, then finally said. "Well, maybe the other books got it wrong."

David threw his hands in the air in exasperation. "You're missing the point. Doesn't it bother you?"

"Not really. I'm a bit curious, but frankly. . ."

David interrupted, stammering, "Well, it bothers me, and it bothers a lot of other people like me. It's hard for some of us to accept facts when they conflict with our beliefs. The facts I learned—information from the books I find most sacred—were inconsistent with my most strongly held beliefs. Maybe it doesn't matter to you. But it matters to me. And facts are facts. You can't just change the facts."

I thought for a moment. "So, change your beliefs."

"No," David said. "That's not how people work."

I shook my head and sighed. What could I say?

David stewed in his seat, unable to respond. I put my hand on his shoulder. "Look, David, I'm sorry. I'm exhausted. A lot is going on right now. I have cancer. Dad just had a stroke. And, according to Danny and everyone around me, the world has turned upside down almost overnight. I can only take in so much at a time."

David sighed. "I know. I'm probably putting too much on you right now. But that's the way it is. C'mon, let's go see Ruby."

As we walked toward the church doors, he said, "You're about to absorb a lot of information. It's all part of something much bigger than either you or me. Please, have patience and listen to Ruby."

I nodded reluctantly. "Sure, David. I'll listen. I'll do that. But I'm telling you, David, I'm tired of all this craziness. I want my old life back, even if it's only for a few days."

+ + +

We walked inside the church where Ruby was waiting, sitting at a small table in the center of a giant room. Three driftwood crosses stood behind her under a dim light. Beside her, an old wooden box rested on the floor.

"Hello, Mel," Ruby said. "I wondered if David could even get you here."

"Good morning, Ruby," I said. "Yes, it's early. And I'm not sure what's going on, but I'm here."

Ruby nodded, looking deep into my eyes. As the silence grew, a chill ran down my back. It was as if Ruby could see my soul. Eventually, she stood up and turned to David. "He's not ready. He might listen, but he doesn't care."

"Please, Ruby, give him a chance," David pleaded.

Ruby turned back to me and grinned. "After all you went through. After all you experienced, you still don't trust me. You are a doubting soul, Mel. You are a skeptical soul."

I stood firm and silent. She was right, but so what, why should I trust her? I barely knew Ruby.

Ruby looked off to the side, thinking, contemplating something to herself. "Is this for better or worse, I don't know. I can't see, but time will tell." After a brief pause, she continued. "Time. It's what we need but don't have. The dark forces are gathering. They are preparing." Ruby turned to me and looked directly into my eyes again. "Some Shadows have already arrived."

At the mention of the Shadows, my eyes opened wide.

Ruby noticed. "Ah! You've seen one. This is a most unfortunate surprise. To happen so soon. Tell me, Mel, did it speak to you?"

I shook my head, half in denial and half in confusion.

Ruby sat back down in her chair. "Please, Mel, sit down. Whether you want to or not, it's time to listen."

Part of me wanted to leave. Part of me wanted to end this wild conversation, but I felt myself sitting down at the table across from Ruby.

She continued, "Tell me about your dreams, Mel. Have you heard the mountain's call? Have you felt its thunder?"

How did she know? I thought.

Ruby, almost surprised, said, "So you have heard it?" She leaned back and continued, almost to herself. "The Shadows have dusted off their drums of war. Their march has surely begun." Then she turned to me and asked, "When did you see the Shadow?"

I hesitated. "The same night I first met you. And I didn't really see it. It was dark and I didn't get a good look."

"This was at your home?" Ruby asked.

"Yes," I said.

She paused for a few moments and then reached into the old box on the floor. "The Shadows will visit you soon. You must set aside your doubts and listen. More than your life depends on it."

Ruby placed a scroll on the table and carefully unrolled it. It was a map of a triangular-shaped island surrounded by three seas. At the top, Latin letters formed the words: "Magna Graecia."

Ruby searched my face. "You know this place, don't you?"

"Yes."

"For too many years, people have forgotten about the importance of this little island. It was once the center of the world."

I nodded.

"But perhaps that is a good thing," Ruby continued. "We wouldn't be sitting here today if others knew what was hidden on that island."

+ + +

Lynn and I had lived in Sicily for three years when I was stationed with the US Navy there. It was where Tyler was born. Knowing that our stay in Sicily was temporary, we explored the island every chance we could. We knew the island well. We loved the island. It was, as Ruby said, a forgotten island. The world had forgotten its history. Sicily had been occupied or inhabited by almost every major civilization in the world. Magna Graecia was its name when it was a part of Greece, over two thousand years ago. Ancient relics still littered its fields. Cities were buried under cities. So, in a way, it came as little surprise to me that something special might be hidden or forgotten on the island of Sicily. Ruby's map had captured my attention.

+ + +

On the map, I saw seven stars. I put my finger on the star near the city of Siracusa and Ruby began to speak. "That's where Paul landed."

"Who?" I asked.

"Paul. The one that was also called Saul. He had two names from two different languages. He sailed into Siracusa after his ship wrecked in Malta during his voyage to Rome.

The ship that took him from Siracusa toward Rome had a figurehead with twin gods on its bow."

"How do you know this?"

"That information is no secret. You'll find it in the book of Acts, toward the end. What's unusual is that it was recorded with such specificity. We believe it was a message to us. We believe that Paul brought an early Codex to Sicily and left it there with instructions to keep it hidden."

I looked down at the map. Stars also marked Catania, Messina, and the Aeolian Islands. There was another near a place called Monreale. Agrigento bore another. These were all places of the ancient Greeks. But it was on Mount Etna where the most prominent mark appeared. Near it, on Etna's southeastern slopes, there was an odd-shaped hill. It was a saddle-like hill with two peaks on its eastern and western sides. Nestled between the two peaks was a small mark of a cross. When my eyes found the mark, I looked up at Ruby.

She smiled. "You know that place, don't you?"

"Yes."

"You know the winding path that leads to the hill."

I nodded.

"You know how it disappears into the woods."

I kept nodding, as if involuntary.

"You know where it leads. You know what it overlooks."

How did she know about this place? The path was hidden, known only to locals. There were no signs. No directions. No information telling others about where it led. On top of that hill, about 10,000 feet above the sea, the hidden path led to one of the most magnificent views of this world. To the south, the sea sparkles and glistens with peace on a clear day. A rainbow of homes and villages dots the mountainside facing the coast.

A giant crater looms to the north, constantly billowing smoke from depths unknown. The peak is dark and charred from fire. A vast, dark lake of hardened lava lies between the hill and the crater. It looks like an ocean was suddenly frozen in time and then painted black. Under the petrified waves, a chaotic tangle of tunnels leads to depths unknown. Everywhere, death lurks. Humans don't enter the caverns. The fragile floors would crack like glass, burying reckless trespassers beneath the rubble.

I knew the hill better than any place in Sicily. Lynn and I had enjoyed picnics on its grassy top. We took Tyler there when we wanted to get away from it all. That hill was our escape.

I looked at Ruby and said, "Yes, I know the place. But how do you?"

"I've been there too, Mel." Ruby leaned toward me. "Mel, you and I have more in common than you think. You'll learn that in time." She paused, then continued, "Sicily is where you've heard the thunder, isn't it?"

"Yes," I said, remembering the once familiar sound of Etna's roar.

Ruby leaned in even closer, almost touching me, and whispered, "It's calling you. This hill. The mountain. The mark. They're calling you."

She was right. I could feel it. But I wanted nothing of it. As if waking from a dream, I shook my head and stood up. "No. I don't want to be a part of this, whatever it is. I just want to go home."

Ruby laughed. "Mel, you are so very predictable. Curiosity alone will keep you here, at least for a few more minutes. Now please, sit down."

Again, she was right. As if under her influence, I found myself sitting at the table again. Despite my yearning to be elsewhere, I couldn't leave.

Ruby continued. "Have you ever heard of a codex?" Ruby asked.

"No," I said.

Before Ruby responded, I noticed that David moved closer to the table. Ruby explained, "A codex is an ancient text, sometimes made from papyrus or other materials. It is the ancestor of the modern book. The Codex is the ancestor of what you call the Bible. Over time, we have discovered several of them and parts of others. Have you heard of the Nicene Council?"

"I think so," I said. At this point, David sat down in a chair beside me.

"Before the Nicene Council, letters were scattered about the world. Mel, for hundreds of years, the letters were in the hands of small, dispersed communities of people. In other words, for hundreds of years after the death of Yeshua, there was no Bible, not as you know it anyway."

David leaned over the table. He began to speak, but Ruby held up her hand. She continued, "Constantine, the Emperor of Rome, sought to change this. He ordered that the Nicene Council be convened. He called religious leaders from across the world to meet in Nicaea and form a consensus—that is, to vote—on the unity of beliefs for this new religion."

"Bishops, if you want to call them by that name, traveled to Nicaea with their letters in hand," she continued. "Many, if not most, wanted their letters to be included. Many wanted their beliefs to be accepted as part of the Codex."

Ruby paused and then said, "But there were others. There were a few who didn't trust Constantine. They feared that he would use their letters to control and oppress the weak. They didn't want their letters in the hands of those who sought power over others. So they kept their letters secret. They formed their own Codex and swore an oath to keep it hidden from the world. They didn't trust the world they lived in. Over time, this group referred to themselves as Custos, Guarda, and other names. The best translation, in English, is Keeper."

Ruby reached back into the old wooden box and removed four more ancient texts, appearing in several different languages, with translations above and below the original text. Ruby arranged them on the table. I reviewed them, and despite my lack of Biblical knowledge, I recognized the texts.

"Do you know what these are?" she asked.

"Books of the Bible," I said. "The four Gospels."

"This is part of the Keepers Codex," Ruby said.

I looked up. I was about to ask her about the rest of the Codex, but David couldn't hold his excitement.

"Mel, isn't this wonderful!" David exclaimed. "We're looking at words from one of the original texts. We're looking at part of one of the lost books of antiquity!"

Yes, I was intrigued. But I didn't share David's joy.

Ruby rolled the text back up and placed them back in the wooden box. "These aren't the only lost books. Others have been found. Are you familiar with the Dead Sea Scrolls? The Gnostic Gospels discovered in Nag Hammadi, Egypt?"

"Not really, but yes I've heard of them," I said.

"Among them, you will find pieces of other Gospels, of Gospels other than the four you know. The Keepers weren't the only ones who hid ancient letters. But the Keepers believe that their Codex contains a lost Gospel that can't be revealed until the time is right. It can only be revealed as a last resort to help save humanity from the dark forces."

Ruby paused. I felt the room around me go dark. Ruby looked at me with her soul-piercing eyes. I felt what I can only describe as a heaviness all around me.

Ruby broke the silence in a low tone, "Keepers are called to duty for reasons unknown. Their existence remains a secret to the visible world. But to the other world—the invisible world—the Keepers are known. They are known by both good and evil forces. Dark forces seek to influence the Keepers. Shadows desire what the Keepers have kept hidden for ages. The world will be in grave danger if the lost book falls into the hands of the Shadows."

Ruby looked at me, gauging whether I understood the significance of what she said.

"All Keepers can sense the Shadows who haunt them. This happens to all Keepers when they are called."

I leaned back and shook my head.

Ruby continued, "Yes, Mel. You have been called."

+ + +

"No," I said, standing up from my chair. "I won't be a part of this."

It was David, not Ruby, who first responded. "Mel, please think about what you're saying. This is not an opportunity of a lifetime. It's an opportunity of . . . of . . . Mel, we're looking at the chance to find something that has been lost for almost 2,000 years!"

"No," I said, then turned to Ruby. "Make David the Keeper. He's the one who cares so much."

David looked at Ruby and shook his head sadly. "It doesn't work that way. I've already asked her. I can't do what you've been called to do."

Ruby smiled. "Keepers are chosen, Mel. You now carry this burden whether you like it or not. What you do with it is your decision. Even the Spirits can't control that."

I sat back down.

Ruby nodded as if she could hear my thoughts.

I folded my arms, leaned back, and asked, "Why me? Why not someone else?"

"Mel," she said. "You have a gift and it's not yours to keep. You must share it with the world."

I shook my head in disbelief. I knew myself well enough to know that I didn't possess any gift extraordinary enough to justify being "chosen" for anything.

"You doubt yourself, Mel," Ruby said. "And, in some ways, that is justified. But you do have a special gift. And other gifts too. To fulfill your duty as a Keeper, you must become self-aware. You must examine your strengths and weaknesses. You must know why you think and act a certain way. Mel, you must understand your individual code."

"My what?" I asked, squinting my eyes in confusion. "Code? Like DNA?"

"Like DNA," Ruby said, leaning closer. "Yes, like DNA, but invisible. It can't be seen under a microscope, but it defines you with the same definiteness as DNA. It shapes your thoughts. It governs your actions. It gives meaning to your decisions." Ruby nodded her head toward David and then said, "It is one reason why David can't attempt what you must do."

Ruby continued, "It's no surprise that you don't believe what I've told you. It's no surprise that you doubt that you've been called. Skepticism is quite natural for you, Mel. It's part of your code. You look for something grounded in objective reason, rather than based on faith, feelings, or beliefs. You seek information, data, and facts.

"But you, Mel, are driven by curiosity. This will drive you to research the things I tell you. That research will show you that I speak the truth, to the extent that the truth can be determined. And you will learn that there is much more that you don't know. You will learn that for centuries others have searched for lost Gospels. And they have found them. You'll learn that the Codex was once as real and definite as any other book or law. You'll learn that knowledge once well-known has been long forgotten and even rejected. Rejected, because the knowledge didn't fit some people's beliefs. You, Mel, are not that way. You seek the truth, even if it hurts. This is part of your code."

Ruby looked at David, who had started nervously pacing. "David is not that way. David makes decisions based on what he believes is true. To David, the Bible and its writings are more than a book of words. To David, the Bible speaks to him. It's as if it can tell him what he needs to hear when he needs to hear it. David doesn't search the Bible for inconsistencies. He searches it for harmony.

"You, Mel, find the inconsistencies curious. They don't offend you or your beliefs. Inconsistencies lead to the truth. That is what you seek, Mel.

"David seeks affirmation. He looks to the Bible to affirm his beliefs. This is part of his invisible code. It is how he is wired. He knows this now. It helps to explain the discomfort he feels when something he hears conflicts with his beliefs. But he does not yearn for the truth like you, Mel.

"The Spirits have called you—not David—to complete this mission. The Spirits need someone who can examine individual passages and see how they fit together naturally. The pieces of this puzzle can't be forced.

"This mission calls for someone who can examine the passages from a distance, putting together words, numbers, and patterns in such a way that completes a vision of what is true and real. David is not equipped for this. His beliefs bend him toward a certain end. Yes, David has very powerful gifts. And they will serve the mission well. But it is you, Mel, who have been called."

Ruby paused, leaned toward me, and again looked deep into my eyes as if she could see my soul.

"Mel, this is what you were put on Earth to do. Think about what I've told you and about what you've seen with your own eyes and heard with your own ears. Examine your own being. Think about what drives you. Think about what you have to offer this world."

Ruby's voice was now low and deep. My eyes closed as she spoke and I felt a hollowness inside of me. I felt small and full of regret at the same time.

Ruby said, "Yes, feel the emptiness. There is an emptiness in all of us. There is a void that needs to be filled. Only a few fortunate souls understand what they were put on Earth to do. To find your purpose is a gift. A gift should not be tossed aside to wither from neglect. Mel, you must answer the call."

I took a deep breath and sighed. It was all too much, happening too soon, but I couldn't ignore all that I had seen, heard, and even felt. When I opened my eyes, I saw an unexpected sight.

A single tear fell from Ruby's face. Her face looked pained, as if she were holding back some great emotion. Her hair seemed a lighter shade of gray.

As she rolled out the map again, Ruby said, "I have carried this burden for many years. It's yours now, Mel." Ruby pointed to the mark of a cross on top of the hill. "It's there. That's where you'll find the book the Keepers have guarded for so many years."

"How do you know?" I asked.

Ruby sighed deeply. "I've seen it, Mel."

Confused, I asked, "So what do you need me for?"

"I couldn't open it." Ruby shook her head slowly. "When I found it, I realized that I was not called to open it. I was called to find it and pass this duty on to the next Keeper."

Ruby rolled up the map and pushed it toward me. "Mel, this is yours now. You must understand that we all have gifts, but you possess an extraordinary gift. You can't see that now. But when you do, you must remember..." Ruby's throat thickened and she couldn't find the words. Another tear dropped from her face. "Mel, you must remember your gift is not yours to keep. You must share it with the world."

All was silent in the room. I looked at the map resting on the table. I didn't want it. I neither understood nor shared Ruby's emotions. It all seemed too odd, too unbelievable. But, then again, the whole world had turned upside down.

Ruby continued, "Take it, Mel. The mountain is calling you. It's a small world and you're only a flight away from the mountain. You're not ready. But with training, you might be able to do what I couldn't."

I shook my head. I knew better than to take the map. Any reasonably objective person would have left the map on the table.

Ruby continued, "Mel, the choice is yours. But either way, the Shadows will haunt you. They want what you are destined to find. No matter what you do, they will haunt you until you leave this world."

I gritted my teeth. Then, half in anger, I reached forward and picked up the map. Ruby nodded, but not with any display of excitement. Even David seemed subdued.

Ruby turned to David and said, "This is enough for one day. Please take him home."

With that, we left. It was a lot to absorb in one morning. As we drove home, I thought, *I need a break from this weird world*. Before we reached my driveway, I dozed off in a dream. Exhausted.

CHAPTER 10

An Unexpected Visitor

For the rest of that day, all proceeded peacefully, almost normally. I spent time with Lynn, Tyler, and Sophia, savoring every moment with them. When I was with my family, I could pretend that the entire world hadn't gone immediately and completely crazy.

In the afternoon, a muggy, warm front pushed the cool air away, which made for a normal winter's day in the low country. I even began to feel normal. It's odd how we can recover so quickly from unusual experiences. I even began to wonder if any of the strange events had happened. Had I dreamt it all?

No. David's persistence wouldn't allow me to deny what had happened that night when we raced across the marsh. I did, however, find comfort in the thought that only a few people knew what had really happened. Few knew about my illness. Few knew about the Spirits. Perhaps, if I focused on the present, I could get through this weirdness one day at a time. Perhaps I could move forward as if nothing remarkably odd had happened.

Then, while Lynn was putting Tyler and Sophia to bed, I heard a voice. It was the same voice I had heard during that awful night. Shivers ran down my spine. His voice was clear and distinctly his, but different than before. Very different from when he was alive. At first, it seemed he sang softly from outside my window:

"Once upon a midnight dreary, while I pondered, weak and weary,
Over many a quaint and curious volume of forgotten lore."

I sat up and looked around, wide awake. He continued, getting louder, singing:

"While I nodded, nearly napping, suddenly there came a tapping,
As of some one gently rapping, rapping at my chamber door."

I saw him in the corner of my room, just a shadow at first. Then his eyes began to glow a greenish, yellowish glow.

Looking at me, still in tune, he said, "'Tis some visitor...tapping at my chamber door—Only this and nothing more."

Stepping from the corner, he appeared as a young man, just as he was when he left this world.

My childhood enemy, a bully to all he knew, Judd Nero, looked at me and said, "It's Poe, you idiot."

"Judd Nero," I said.

"Judd? That name is dead. I go by Nero now," he said, then walked around, casually looking at the stuff cluttering my room. "I'm in Poe's division."

"What do you want?"

"Oh, nothing," he said. "Or everything. It's all the same to me. You really should meet him. I think you would get along quite well."

"What is this about?" I asked.

"Edgar. Allan. Poe, you fool. Abandoned by his father. Cursed by doubt and heartache. Talk about a tortured soul. Did you know he died sick and alone in a gutter? Tragic. Makes my life look like an absolute joy, I'd say." Nero moved about my room, still in a casual manner. Then he added, "But he is not forgotten. Not yet."

Nero's presence angered me. I wanted him gone. Immediately and forever gone. But before I could say anything, he continued, "You might as well get used to me being around. I've been assigned to you. Isn't it wonderful?"

I looked at him, confused. He smiled, delighting in the darkness. "Mel, listen to this—I'm now your protector, your bodyguard." He paused but held his wide smile. "Aren't you the fortunate one?"

Unable to restrain his amusement, he slowly danced around the room.

This should have annoyed me, but I remembered the earlier night across the marsh, when Nero's spirit appeared as a boy weeping. I said, "I'm sorry about what happened. I know we've never been friends, but…"

"Sorry!" he said, almost giddy. "Mel, I came here to *thank* you! And I also came here under specific instructions from the Dark One, but, as far as I'm concerned, I came here to thank you, Mel. You freed me!"

"Freed you?" I asked. "From what?"

"From what? From this world and all its juvenile silliness! From the torture of eyes everywhere, always looking down on me. From my father and his cold heart. And from all the other awful woes of this world. I'm free! And Mel, I can help free you too. Not in the way you helped me, but in something more unusual. Something more real and immediate." He picked up a small glass globe that was sitting on my desk. "Mel, you could be free here on Earth, walking like a god among mortals. Would you like that? Would you like me to free you from all your human weaknesses?"

"Nero," I said. "I really wish you would just leave me alone."

"No, sir." Nero shook his head. "The Dark One won't allow that. But don't worry. You wouldn't worry if you could see the world as I do now."

Nero found a chair and sat down, our eyes now even. He asked, "Mel, do you know what my problem was?"

I thought about the long list of evils that had plagued him over the years. His mother. His father. His station in life.

"None of those," he said, somehow seeing my thoughts. "My problem, above all other problems, was this: I cared. I cared way too much, which means anything more than not caring at all. I cared about what my mother thought. I cared about what my father thought. I cared about what you and all the other poor beasts on this planet thought. But death purged me of all those stupid, ridiculous human feelings. They're all gone now, washed away in a flash. And it happened so fast! When I arrived, other Shadows couldn't believe it. It takes some Shadows eons to rid themselves of the silly feelings and sentimental notions that hold humans back. Listen to this: Hitler—*the* Adolf Hitler—is in my division too. Yet after all these years, he's but a private, the lowest of ranks. He's a baby of a Shadow, still a prisoner to all the insecurities that warped his sad, lonely life. While I—a poor kid from Camden—lost my insecurities in a flash. My promotion was immediate. What fun it was to watch the envy ripple among the Shadows! No one before me met the Dark One on his very first night. It's the reason, I think, why he assigned me to you. Isn't that outstanding?"

Nero looked at me but didn't expect a response. Nor did I have one. Something, some afterlife experience, had transformed Nero's speech and mannerisms. He was no longer crude and rough. Instead, he walked and talked as if he had knowledge beyond my understanding and beyond the understanding of all others. And this, I would soon learn, was true.

"You'll change your mind," Nero said. "I'll help you with that. I'll help you with a lot of things. Mel, when you see the world as I do, you'll be able to move about freely too, not like me, in a mostly invisible way, but as a human in the flesh here on Earth."

"Nero," I said angrily, "I will never be like you."

"Oh, stop it," Nero said, waving his hand dismissively in the air. "That's weakness speaking. Your problem, Mel, is that you still care. And I bet you think others care too. Give me some time and I'll rid you of those notions. You have never truly died before, not fully, not in the way known only to us Shadows. You are halfway there, with one foot in and one foot out. Mel, you should consider your condition a blessing. Few get that chance. The rumors are that none have had the chance that will soon be yours. There is a path for you, if you so choose, to a destiny unavailable to all others. Mel, if you could see what I see and mingle with the Shadows I know, then you would understand that I am serious when I tell you that it is a true honor for me to serve you."

I wanted him to stop talking and to leave. I hated him more than ever before. But he continued, "I'm afraid there's no time for all this brotherly love. We have work to do. Very important work. I'm still in training, as are you."

I flinched. Nero stopped moving long enough to absorb my reaction. I thought about Ruby and what she had told me.

"Ah!" he said, "I have hit the mark. Yes, I know about Ruby and the pitiful Pastor David. They are necessary parts of your destiny—*our* destiny. You should listen to them, Mel. The Dark One insists that I not interfere with their work. We Shadows have no power over certain matters. You, at the moment, are protected by both sides, a very unusual luxury."

My head was spinning. "I don't understand."

"You will," Nero said. "But for now, you should carry on as you wish. I have dropped in mainly to let you know that exciting times await us. Don't worry about your little life or your precious little family. You'll be ok now that you're under the protection of the Dark One. Few ever get that honor."

I still didn't understand what he was talking about. I said nothing, but he knew. Almost laughing, he said, "If you could understand but a fraction of what all this means, Mel, you could rule the world! Think about what you could do if you moved about without fear or anxiety. Think of what you could accomplish if you didn't care about all those around you!"

Nero moved back toward the dark corner where he first appeared. "Mel, eventually you will realize that you don't matter. You will see that nobody cares. Nobody will ever care about how you feel or what is important to you. Nobody cares about your ideas or your thoughts. Nobody cares about how much money you have. Nobody cares about whatever happiness or joy you find in this world. People don't care about you. They care about one thing above all else: themselves. This you will soon understand. And death won't change that. After you die, people will go on with their lives. They will forget you. A generation will pass, and you will be forgotten. Time buries everything, Mel. Nobody cares. Isn't it wonderful!"

Nero grinned and danced a bit more until his shadow began to fade. Then he looked at me and said, "Don't worry, Mel, I will return."

Nero began to sing, reciting Poe's old poem, "Ah, distinctly I remember, it was in the bleak December; And each separate dying ember wrought its ghost upon the floor."

Nero's shadow half disappeared, but I could still hear him in the night.

"Eagerly I wished the morrow;—vainly I had sought to borrow.
From my books surcease of sorrow—sorrow for the lost *world*—For the rare and radiant One whom *some angels called our Lord*—Nameless *here* for evermore!"

And with that, he was gone.

CHAPTER 11

A New Dawn

Nero's return had haunted me throughout the night, long after he left. Sleep evaded me, and I remained restless. But as the sun rose the next morning, my anxiety faded. The sun seemed to wash away most of my worries.

Rubbing my eyes, I walked into our living room where Lynn stood at the stove, armed with a spatula. She had fixed a fantastic spread—buttermilk pancakes with maple syrup, fresh blueberries and strawberries, scrambled eggs with cheese, and more. I said, "Wow! What's the occasion?"

She didn't turn around or even change her position in the slightest. Without hesitation, she replied, "My birthday."

"Oh . . ."

"Anything else?"

"I'm so sorry. Have I been out of it for that long? What can I do?"

"Well, you can start by taking a break from this midlife crisis thing. I've given it enough time and I think you should be done with it. I'm tired and the kids will be up soon. Here, finish cooking my breakfast."

It took only a few seconds for me to emerge from my fog. Trying to see the situation from her eyes, I wondered, *How did she do it? How had she put up with my jackassery for so long?*

While it started off rocky, Lynn's birthday marked the beginning of the best two months of my life. That's how I see them now, anyway, especially when contrasted with the days before and after those two great months. I think we need contrast to show us how good we once had it.

I needed someone like Lynn to pull me from the fog. And that's precisely what she did for me. With help from her no-nonsense and practical ways, I gradually began to feel a sense of normalcy, if we can call it that.

On the morning of Lynn's birthday, I realized I had to tell her about the diagnosis. She deserved to know about my cancer.

As I thought about how to tell her the news, I nearly ruined breakfast. I burnt everything I cooked. I dropped forks, spoons, and plates. Then I spilled her milk. Finally, as I was haphazardly wrecking the kitchen, Lynn walked over and touched my arm. Looking up at me, she said, "Let's go outside."

As we sat down in a couple of rocking chairs on our porch, I tried to find the words. But my throat thickened and my eyes began to water. I was like a child, brokenhearted and confused. It was Lynn who began the conversation.

"You can tell me when you're ready."

I nodded, still unable to speak. Looking straight ahead—I couldn't look her in the eyes—I said, "Lynn, I have cancer."

Those words were surprisingly hard to say, but I felt an immediate relief when I told her.

Lynn moved her chair next to mine and put her hand on my arm. At first, she didn't say anything. She didn't fall to pieces in a mess. She didn't break down and cry. Instead, she took a deep breath and continued to rock back and forth, never letting go of my arm.

I continued. "Dr. Manning says it's all over my body. He says it's a miracle I'm still walking and talking."

Lynn listened while I talked. "I don't understand it. So much has happened during these past few days. I don't even feel that bad. A bit foggy, but I feel ok."

Lynn nodded again, then she stopped. "Could he be wrong?"

I looked at her. "I don't think so. Dr. Manning seemed so confident after seeing the images."

Lynn squeezed my arm and said, "We'll get through this."

Her strength was amazing. Her steadiness was almost contagious. Lynn didn't jump to the worst-case scenario. She didn't immediately embrace fear. She saw the situation for what it was at the moment, not for what it might be. We were different in this way. As we rocked arm-in-arm, I began to realize that Lynn would be ok. I might not make it. But Lynn would remain grounded. She would keep Tyler and Sophia grounded too. God, the world needs more people like Lynn. The world needs more people who don't immediately scatter in fear of bad news. The world needs steady souls like Lynn. It was one of her gifts. It was part of her invisible code.

While rocking in her chair, Lynn said, "You know, I just read a story about a guy who had cancer and moved to Sicily. He changed his diet and changed his whole way of life. His cancer went away. Doctors couldn't explain it."

Lynn's mention of Sicily caught me off guard. Did she know about Ruby? Was this a sign? An invitation to tell her everything?

I considered telling her about Ruby, but couldn't do it. I had dropped enough bombs for one day, so I just half laughed and said, "Yeah, maybe we should move back to Sicily."

Lynn turned to me and said, "I would do that if that's what you wanted to do."

Wow, I thought. Such impulsiveness was not Lynn's way. But she was serious. I smiled and squeezed her hand.

Our short conversation did wonders for my anxiety. I felt refreshed and ready to take on the day. I felt comfort in knowing Lynn would be ok.

As these thoughts filled my mind, Lynn said, "Remember Jen?"

"From college?" I asked.

"Yes," she said. "When Jen's mother got cancer, the doctor said, 'Whatever you do, don't look at the Internet. Don't look at the odds. Some people do beat the odds and we don't know why.'"

And with that, I began to feel a small but real glimmer of hope.

For the next two months, Nero stayed away and no other Shadows haunted me. I set aside most of the "Keeper" business. It was David who wouldn't let go of it. He pestered me without end. I, however, ignored most of his ramblings about me being "chosen" as one of the "Keepers." David persisted with such enthusiasm that I thought he was reverting to his old, mad ways. I could not, however, deny that he was always sincere.

I credit most of my joy during those two months to the first phase of nearly dying. During the first phase, you treat every moment, every second, as if it is precious, as if it might be your last and you can never get those moments back again. You hold your loved ones tighter. You pay attention to the little things. Things your kids do and say become treasures, unrivaled in value to anything else here on Earth. You feel this way, of course, because all of that is true.

During the first phase of nearly dying, you live more in the present and you notice details, which is not like me to do. But it pays off, allowing you to see things that you might have otherwise missed.

Sophia, even at the age of three, was a singer. I knew this. This observance could not escape even the worst of fathers. But in my heightened state of awareness, I paid extra attention to the moments when she snuck outside to sing and dance. She always did this alone, never with an audience, not one she could see.

During those two wonderful months, I caught myself spying on her performances. I would quietly hide in a corner or open a window to hear her songs. Oh, how beautiful it was to watch! To see a child so happy in her own joy. I did not, however, always get away unscathed.

When she detected my presence, she would immediately cease her beautiful singing, stomp her foot, and give me the grump face.

Do you know the grump face? Not all children can pull it off. Sophia would squint her eyes, pout her lips, and contort every muscle in her face to forcefully convey the message that the grump face was not happy. Of course, when confronted with the grump face, it was all I could do not to laugh, which naturally caused the grump face to storm off in a huff.

As I sit in this bell tower in Sicily, I miss that grump face. I'd give anything to see it again. Sophia was precious in other ways too. Every now and then, she would speak in a different language—one she had created. It was a song-like language delivered in rhythm and rhyme. She would speak it when answering even the most basic of questions.

Here's what our conversations sounded like.

If I asked, "Sophia, how are you doing?"

She might respond, "Nimbily bimbily,"

If I inquired further, she'd respond, "Hubbaly bubbaly," or, "Jibbily bibbily."

I would get a similar response if I asked her about her day.

"How was your day, Sophia?"

"It was nibbily."

Her musings also took the shape of poetry, at times. Not the kind of poetry that would win a Pulitzer Prize. It was far better than that. And effortless too.

If I was lucky, I might hear about a mumbling moose with aardvark toes, who may or may not have a nubbily nose. It would mibble about with stops and starts, powered by incredible nozzle farts.

She produced the kind of magic that no adults can perform. It was pure and untainted by time. Reflecting on her songs makes me wonder—when do we lose our ability to imagine and to create in the ways we once could as children?

Sophia could still tap into that magic. She had access to the sacred source, whatever it was. The sad part is that I've forgotten much of what she said. My brain couldn't retain it in a way I could share with you now, which made her songs even more precious.

Like a mist of vapor, her musings seemed to evaporate as quickly as they had been brought to life. Yet I was too dense to capture them—too short-sighted to write them down.

With cancer on my heels, I was living in the moment, savoring every second. The fact that her musings were just for me brightened the magic. During those solitary, private performances, I could see Sophia's gifts.

Every child is different, of course, each with their own unique gifts. I believe this with all of my heart and mind. Every child has a gift. Looking back on those times, I now realize that it was my job—our job as parents, teachers, coaches, and adults who give a damn—to help our children find their gifts. And then to nurture those gifts before time extinguishes the fire that burns inside of them.

Sophia's gift was apparent. She could sing like a bird among the trees. Tyler, however, had a very different gift. He could see patterns. Tyler could process information, especially numbers, and rearrange them in ways that were almost, if not actually, superhuman. And he could remember it all too. It was as if his brain were a supercomputer.

Tyler got the memory part from my father and from my grandfather too. As for his gift with numbers, he got that from all directions. It was part of his invisible code.

I was decent in math and I enjoyed working with numbers, but I was nothing compared to Tyler.

His abilities far exceeded mine. Tyler enjoyed solving problems as another kid might enjoy playing ball. He loved it. And he couldn't get enough.

At the age of two, Tyler could read. That's what Danny thought, anyway. During one of Danny's visits, Tyler picked up the book *Goodnight, Goodnight, Construction Site* and recited the first page perfectly without missing a single word. He turned to the second page—same thing. Meanwhile, Danny watched over Tyler's shoulder.

When Tyler was halfway through *Goodnight, Goodnight, Construction Site*, Danny started shaking his head. Then Danny stood up and began to pace. Finally, he walked over to me and raised his hands in disbelief. "Holy Bleep!! Your kid can Bleeping read! He's only two and he can read!"

I calmly responded, "Danny, Tyler can't read."

"I just saw him read every word on every page. This is ridiculous!"

"Danny, he can't read."

Still pacing back and forth, Danny couldn't make sense of it. He knew enough to know that kids Tyler's age can't read. And the truth was this: Tyler couldn't read.

The reality was Tyler had an incredible, computer-like memory. Lynn and I had read him the book at bedtime and without us realizing it, he memorized the words that went with each page.

When Tyler was five, he learned to solve a Rubik's Cube. I spent hours trying to mimic Tyler's motions, but I still couldn't solve it. I watched in awe as Tyler shifted the cube at lightning speed. Tyler's little fingers moved about as if he were swiftly typing on a keyboard. Tyler recognized the patterns and memorized what pieces needed to move until all the colors aligned. Once he figured it out, he repeated the process over and over until he could solve the cube in less than a minute.

I once saw Tyler shuffle the cube and mix it up again after solving it. Tyler studied each side of the mixed-up cube carefully, then he put the cube behind his back, where his fingers again went to work. A few seconds later, Tyler placed the cube down in front of him. It was in perfect form.

Somewhere inside of Tyler's brain, a supercomputer churned. That was special enough. But there was more to Tyler than that. There was something else residing in him. It was supernatural, perhaps something spiritual, if you can describe it that way. Something gave balance to the computer that churned in Tyler's brain. I can't explain it with words, but perhaps you can see it in how Tyler treated others.

In preschool, Tyler often played alone. He walked around the playground examining the toys and structures, digging for small treasures, and building miniature forts. He often kept to himself and we wondered, at times, if he was aware of those who played around him. It wasn't that he didn't enjoy being around others. He seemed to be friends with all. As one of his preschool teachers explained, "Tyler's doing fine. He's friends with everyone, even the villains."

In the middle of one year in preschool, a girl named Olivia joined his class. Olivia's family was in the military. Like many military kids, she was expected to come in and out of town. Even young children understood, at some level, the nature of that transient lifestyle. Military children and their parents are often new to a town, which means they don't enjoy the benefits and social conveniences of having lifelong friends and family nearby. And a small town adds emphasis to this nomadic reality.

On Olivia's first day at recess, she walked around the playground but no other children would play with her. It wasn't that she was weird or socially distant, it was because others sensed that she was just passing through. Eventually, Olivia sat down at a picnic table, alone, watching the other children play.

Tyler noticed. He went over to the table and sat next to her. He didn't say anything. He didn't need to. Both Tyler and Olivia sat there watching the other children play. Then it happened. It was the sort of thing adults would never do. Teenagers would be too afraid. But Tyler, a preschooler at the time, put his hand on Olivia's hand and held it. And for the rest of recess, they sat at the little table, hand-in-hand.

These were the moments that made us love Tyler so much. There was something wonderful inside of him. Something brave. Something very human, but also something beyond our understanding.

I was never a genius. I often wondered what made some people smarter than others. How could some people process information and understand it at a rate far faster than others? Why were some born to sing? Others to paint? Others to dance? Others to lead? From where did such blessings flow?

We all have a gift. We all have a zone where we are completely comfortable and dialed into what we're doing.

I could see Sophia's gift. I could see Tyler's gift. According to Ruby, I had to find mine.

CHAPTER 12

The End of an Era

When did you find these letters, anyway? I wonder if your generation will struggle with issues similar to those we faced during the year that won't be mentioned. I wonder if the Shadows can influence millions of humans in almost an instant, preying on our invisible code. I wonder where you look to find reliable information.

If you found these letters soon after the pandemic, you know exactly what life was like before and after it hit. We don't get many moments in history that change our way of life like that almost overnight. 9/11, maybe. Pearl Harbor, probably.

And yet, talking about the pandemic was almost taboo in many settings. Discussing seemingly benign issues could release an explosion of emotion. Issues like: Whether to wear a mask. Whether to stand six feet away from your neighbor. Whether to shake another's hand. People drew lines on these matters and somehow tied them to politics. The tension was high. But why?

Then there was the death count. We were losing thousands of lives to the pandemic. Let's see if I can put it in perspective. At Pearl Harbor, over 2,400 Americans died. In all of WWII, we lost about 420,000 Americans. Vietnam took about 60,000 American lives. On 9/11, just under 3,000 perished. The wars in Iraq and Afghanistan combined claimed just over 7,000 deaths of U.S. service members. In the following years, over 30,000 service members committed suicide. Even conservative estimates concluded that the pandemic claimed over 1 million American lives. During much of that awful year, America experienced, by death count, a Pearl Harbor almost every day.

And yet, many believed that COVID was a hoax. To some, it was simply a bad cold. Others took unnecessarily extreme measures to protect themselves. It is human nature to want certainty, to want answers. But, in the beginning, no one understood COVID, not the novel coronavirus that plagued our world. Confusion reigned, spilling over onto almost everything. People didn't trust the government. People didn't trust each other. People didn't trust the data. Here's the thing: Should you?

Should you trust the information I gave you? You don't know me, and at this point, I'm almost certainly dead. To verify these numbers, you must compare them to data from reliable sources. You must set aside time to do your own research. You must examine the information with a critical mind, independent of what you want to believe. Can you do that?

Many can't, or at least, they don't. Some don't take the time. Some are offended by information if it is inconsistent with their beliefs. They look for information that affirms what they believe. It's part of their invisible code. It's part of being human. And the Shadows love this.

The Shadows understand our invisible code. They understand how humans are programmed to think. They know that most humans believe what they want to believe. They know that humans do what they want to do. If you could see the world as the Shadows do, then the year that brought the pandemic makes perfect sense. Yes, the virus caused unimaginable damage. But there was a more destructive force at work. It was another invisible force far more insidious than the virus itself. And more lasting too. The Shadows know this force. And they wielded it with great effectiveness that year. The Shadows reeled in joy as their efforts to turn friends and family against one another succeeded like never before.

The pandemic brought widespread fear, chaos, and confusion. But this was just the beginning. Extraordinary powers converged to create conditions where the Shadows enjoyed unprecedented influence over humans. We weren't ready for it. But the Shadows had been preparing for this moment in time.

+ + +

As I sit in this bell tower, I still long for the two months of joy after Christmas. Those were wonderfully precious days. In these dark hours, I need those memories like a car needs fuel. Like all good things, those days came to an end.

After I saw the data of COVID's spread, I told Dad, "You're going to be very busy. Very busy for a long time."

Even Dad, who understood numbers and exponential growth, didn't expect it to happen so rapidly. Nor did he, or anyone else, think that Camden would become the epicenter in the South. New York took the hardest hit first. The sheer density of its population provided fertile ground for the virus to spread.

Camden is a small town nestled in the middle of the relatively small state of South Carolina. Dad steadily performed his duties as the city manager. He focused on the customary issues of a town—utilities, roads, parks, schools, and local businesses. No towns—big or small—had a manual on how to deal with a worldwide pandemic.

To complicate matters, Dad was having seizures, which we thought were from his stroke. That's what the doctors told us.

Most of Asia knew what was coming. They had dealt with widespread respiratory viruses before. They had worn masks before. They had quarantined before. America had little recent experience with this. Such things were not on our radar.

If any of us learned anything during the pandemic, it was this: We are lousy at predicting human behavior. But I know this—grave mistakes are made when we treat others the way we want to be treated, when we assume that others want what we want, and when we assume that others think the way we think. It's as if the golden rule has set us all up. The rule doesn't always work, especially in times of stress and chaos. When the golden rule backfires, it leaves us shocked at the behavior of others, even people we thought we knew well.

The pandemic brought stress and chaos to a population unprepared, leaving scars on almost everyone. All the while, the Shadows smiled.

CHAPTER 13

Nero Returns

There are few things in this world more destructive than the firm belief that one is right. Think of the leaders who have waged wars because they believed they were right. Think of the friends and family members who have hurt their loved ones because they believed they were right. None of us are immune. I wonder how much healing would occur if we paused to think, "Maybe I was wrong." What if we chose to listen with real curiosity rather than respond with anger and stubbornness? Oh, the places we might go! Curiosity, however, did not reign in the year that won't be mentioned. Our thoughts were overshadowed by the influence of dark, invisible forces.

I didn't understand this at first and probably never would have but for Ruby and, as much as it hurts to admit, Nero.

Everyone had their own struggles. Mine, for much of the year, centered around Dad. His seizures didn't stop. They progressed in both frequency and duration. No one knew why. My health, however, seemed to improve, another mystery.

Dad's doctors continued to treat him as if he'd suffered a stroke. For months, he took strong, powerful medications to no effect. And all this happened when COVID struck Camden.

This presented unusual challenges for Camden, for us, and for Dad.

To manage the arrival of COVID, Dad and his staff set up what looked very much like a command center. They developed a battle rhythm (that's what we called it in the military) where they met each day to assess the situation, examine their plan, and then execute that plan. As if at war, the leaders of Camden maintained regular communication with the Governor, other state leaders, and the press. Televised press briefings from Camden became the norm.

Camden was a small town unaccustomed to such attention. People were scared and anxious. National politics took a nasty turn and people seemed to lose their minds. Threats came from every direction.

Dad brought a steady voice to it all. While everyone had their own opinions, Dad had to make the tough decisions. His presence calmed those around him. But I knew that too could change in an instant. During every press conference, I cringed and gripped my hands, wondering if a seizure might take hold of Dad while on air. They always hit unexpectedly.

Dad didn't know it, but his duties during that time resembled, almost exactly, the duties of a military commander in combat. I understood the world of combat. I understood the stress, the burdens, and the sleepless nights that come with that kind of battle rhythm. Dad had never served in such times, but you would have never known it. He was a natural. He was in his zone.

When Camden was under siege—by both COVID and other invisible forces—I found myself in the unique position of having a seat next to Dad, Camden's commander. I got to see what he saw and hear what he heard.

During the shutdown, the world had become such an odd place that I had all but forgotten about Nero's visit and his promise to return. Only David's persistence kept that memory alive. David continued to plead with me to meet with Ruby. He kept saying that I had to continue my training. He said that time was getting shorter, that the Shadows were gathering and their influence was spreading. He kept talking about how I had to "find my zone." David pestered me to the point where I thought he was losing his mind all over again. Then, during a moonless night while Lynn was putting our children to bed, I heard a tap, tap, tapping at my window.

From the other side, Nero sang:

"And the silken, sad, uncertain rustling of each dark curtain
Thrilled me—Filled me with fantastic terrors never felt before;
So that now, to still the beating of my heart, I stood repeating
'Tis some visitor entreating entrance at my chamber door—
Some late visitor entreating entrance at my chamber door;
This it is and nothing more."

Then he appeared.
"Hello, Nero," I said.
"Hello, Mel," he said. "I've missed you too."
"Poe again?" I asked.
"You do listen," he said. "Now, let's get to our business. Have you been enjoying this new, dark world and all that we've done with it? Isn't it beautiful?"
"Isn't *what* beautiful?"
"The kickoff, the launch, the beginning of what must happen," Nero said. "I do say that even I didn't expect fear to take hold so suddenly and spread so quickly. There has been nothing quite like it in the history of time, my fellow Shadows say."
I remained silent, half understanding what he said.
"Oh yes, Mel. This is all the devil's work. We—the dark forces—are in our zone," Nero said, pausing long enough to gauge my reaction. I remained poker-faced, but he saw through it.
Nero grinned and then continued, "You'll come around, Mel. You have to. The Dark One insists."

Nero eased over to the side of my bed and sat on its corner. "Mel, don't you wonder why the world is going mad? Don't you wonder, even a tiny bit, why all of this is happening? Or do you believe that it is all simply a random coincidence? Do you truly believe that this all started with a man and a dead bat at a wet market in China?"

Nero laughed. "I do wish you could have joined me during *my* training. The Dark One believes that you have great potential. But, of course, you're not one of us. Not yet. I must say, it would open your eyes to see what I've seen. If you knew but a fraction of what I've learned, then you would have influence far beyond that of all other mortals. And it's so beautifully simple too. I kick myself for having missed it when I was alive. Mel, I could have had it all."

Nero eased closer and looked me in the eyes. Then he asked, "Have you enjoyed *your* training sessions?"

I didn't respond. I didn't need to.

"Ah!" Nero said. "You've declined Ruby's offer. I should have known. Oh, how she and the pitiful Pastor David must be worried. But they shouldn't. You'll come around. You'll listen to Ruby. No amount of denial or procrastination can stop the inevitable, especially when us Shadows help push it along."

Nero paused, thinking to himself. Then he asked, "Has Ruby told you about the invisible code?"

"You mean, the Codex?" I asked.

"No, not that old relic," Nero said. "I'm talking about the invisible human code. It's what controls all of you silly beasts. You certainly are missing out, Mel. But, of course, that's expected of someone who thinks like you. It's part of your code. You're not the type to make a leap of faith unless it's grounded in fact and reason. Let me try to speak your language, Mel. You see, humans are binary creatures, little more than walking, talking clumsy computers. You're programmed with 0's and 1's. Or would you rather me say,

Yes's and No's or Do's and Don'ts. You pick one side or the other—Good or Bad, Right or Wrong. It has always been this way, Mel. Even as I speak, your brain is trying to make sense of me. It wants to know if I am good or bad. If I am here to help or harm. Whether I should stay or go. Humans don't like the area in between. Confusion and uncertainty make you uncomfortable. You prefer to reside in the Black or White, but it's in the Gray where us Shadows dwell. That's where we Shadows thrive. All Shadows know the invisible human code. It's what gives us our influence over you."

"I don't understand," I said.

"You will," Nero said. "I know you, Mel. I know how you think. I know that you'll come to understand what I'm saying. You, Mel, can set aside your feelings and search for the truth. The truth drives you, even if you hear something contrary to what you believe. This makes you different from those who stop listening when someone offends their feelings. Not you, Mel. Curiosity compels you to listen. That's part of your code. And I want you to know the code. I want you to understand it. I want you to listen to the voice inside of you. Mel, listen to the voice that's calling you. It wants you to climb that mountain. It wants you to retrieve what's waiting to be found. It wants you to reveal what must be revealed to all of us. We must know what has been hidden for far too long. The world deserves to know."

Nero paused, just long enough for me to absorb what he said. Then he continued, "Mel, I know what Ruby seeks. We seek it too. It's the reason that I've been assigned to you."

"Look, Nero. I don't want to have anything to do with it. I'm not going to be a part of whatever . . ."

"Oh, but you will!" Nero interrupted. "You're already a part of it. Think about what you've already seen and heard. Listen to the voice inside of you—the one that does not lie. It's calling you, Mel. You must put aside your worldly worries and answer that call. If you knew what depended on your efforts, then you would race up that mountain and retrieve it right now."

"Do it yourself," I said.

"Oh, I would if I could, Mel," Nero said. "But no. That's beyond the powers of us Shadows, perhaps even beyond that of the Nephilim and their descendants. That duty is reserved for a human, an ordinary human like yourself. It has always been that way."

Confused, I looked at Nero.

"So you really don't know," Nero said. "You really haven't begun your training. Mel, you must heed Ruby's plea. You must go to her. And when you do, ask her about the Nephilim. Ask her about the other gods. Ask her about us Shadows."

Nero began moving back toward the window. Before vanishing, he said, "I'll return. You will learn to trust in what I say. In three days, we will open the gates. You'll have a front-row seat and I will sit next to you. So much will be destroyed. Old wounds will be opened. Good people will turn on one another. And by the way, Camden—that little town of ours—the Dark One has selected it to burn. You and I will get to see it burn. Isn't that splendid!"

Nero smiled and then began singing Poe's song again:

"Presently my soul grew stronger; hesitating then no longer,
'Sir,' said I, 'or Madam, truly your forgiveness I implore;
But the fact is I was napping, and so gently you came rapping,
And so faintly you came tapping, tapping at my chamber door,
That I scarce was sure I heard you'—here I opened wide the door;
Darkness there and nothing more."

As Nero finally faded from my view, he said, "He was one of them, you know?"

"Who?" I asked.

"Poe," Nero said. "He was a descendant, linked to the line of the Nephilim. Diluted, but still linked. Do you actually think a human mind could create what he brought to this world? No, such beautiful darkness comes from somewhere else. Mel, ask her about us. Ask Ruby about where it comes from. Ask her about Einstein and Beethoven and Da Vinci and all the others who left their mark on this world. You have a gift, Mel. The time has come for you to share it. It's not yours to keep."

Then he continued singing Poe's poem:

"Deep into that darkness peering, long I stood there wondering, fearing. Doubting, dreaming dreams no mortal ever dared to dream before!"

And then he was gone.

CHAPTER 14

My Zone

If you knew me well, then you would understand why I felt confused after Nero left my room. Some of what he said made sense, but the part about me having a gift that amounted to anything meaningful was absurd. I'm not very good at anything. I have no artistic talent. I'm not organized. And I find it incredibly difficult to focus on even the simplest of tasks. If I'm good at anything, it's starting something and not finishing it. My life is riddled with unfinished projects.

Nero, however, had said enough to make me curious, so I decided to give Ruby a chance. I would meet with her again and share with her what Nero had said.

When I told Pastor David I would meet with Ruby, he was beside himself with excitement. On our way to his church, he seemed like a kid on the way to Disney World. "Oh, this is wonderful! You're doing the right thing, Mel. I promise."

I didn't share his joy.

+ + +

Ruby and I met again at the round table in the dimly lit sanctuary. I had not seen her since the day she told me about the Nicene Council and the lost letters.

After I took my seat at the table, Ruby asked, "How is your father?"

"He's doing ok," I said, a bit surprised by the inquiry.

She nodded. "I think of him often," Ruby said. "He is a good man."

"Yes," I said.

"How is Lynn?"

"She's fine. She's always doing fine."

"Yes, Lynn is a rock, Mel," Ruby said. "She's the rock of your family."

"I know."

"And she let you come here, without any questions?" Ruby asked.

"Yes, she didn't ask much."

"Where did you tell her you were going?" Ruby asked.

"Sunday school."

Ruby laughed.

"Yeah," I said. "That's what she did too."

"She trusts you," Ruby said. "You'll need that trust."

"She's seen the lowest of my lows. This isn't it."

"Good," Ruby said. "Now let's begin."

Ruby closed her eyes and slowly reached for my hands.

"What are you doing?" I said, pulling my hands back. "I came to tell you about Nero."

"In due course. Trust me, Mel. Close your eyes. Reach out and touch my hands. Breathe, Mel."

When I touched Ruby's fingers, a tingle ran up my arms and down my spine. The hair on my head felt as if it stood straight.

"Breathe," she said slowly. "Listen to your breath as you inhale and exhale. Become one with the present. Listen with your mind. Feel the sensations around you. Breathe."

In a few moments, I began to relax. Soon, I felt myself drift off into a meditative state.

Ruby whispered, "Let go of your worries. Let go of your fears. Breathe. Clear your mind."

As she spoke, a weight seemed to lift from my shoulders. I felt lighter and almost transparent.

Ruby continued, "Take your mind back to when you were a child, when you ran free in this world, unencumbered by any burdens. Run free with the friends of your youth. Now, remember what it was you loved most as a child. Go, find that place. Find your zone."

+ + +

This must all sound odd to you, in whatever year you found my letters. Understand, it was odd to me too. I was unfamiliar with meditation and the visions it can produce. But Ruby was a master. It took little effort for her to induce a trance and take me back to my childhood.

At first, I was running through a tall pine forest with my childhood dog, Duchess, by my side. Duchess would jump and bite the bark from trees. It was a silly thing for me to run wild with her through the woods. But we were as happy and free as the animals of the wild.

I hadn't seen Duchess in almost two decades, but she appeared as clear and alive as she had been in her youth. My memory of her had not faded a shade, probably because she had been with me during almost all of my childhood.

She wandered up to our house when I was almost five. I didn't have a brother, so when I explored the nearby woods, it was Duchess who went along. She learned how to catch a football and bring it back, or not, depending on the game. At the end of the day when Mom called my name, it was Duchess who led the way. For the next 16 years, we were the best of friends. She was unconditionally loyal to the very end.

If you've ever loved an animal with all your heart, then perhaps you have wondered if it too had a soul. I don't wonder. Not anymore. During college over the winter break, our time together came to an end, which is the way of all good things.

I had been busy at school and didn't even think to come home to see her. I certainly didn't realize how sick she was. I got in late on Friday and woke up early Saturday morning to go hunting with a friend. Duchess saw me move toward the door and crawled across the floor toward me, dragging her hindlegs because her hips had failed. She looked up at me and, with more clarity than any human language, she spoke to me with her eyes.

I don't cry in front of my friends. But as I picked Duchess up in my arms, tears fell fast down my face. I knew what she wanted me to do. Holding her gently, I carried her outside and walked along a path lined with pines. Her snaggle-toothed grin told me she could see, smell, and feel everything around her. We were together again, for one last time, walking in the woods where we had often wandered.

I carried her through the trees up a hill where we had played as children. It was her favorite place, full of scrubby bushes and brambles where rabbits and other creatures would hide. As we approached the top of the hill, I could feel her breathe against my chest. Her eyes said, "Thank you" and "I love you." I held on tighter, washing her with my tears. Oh, how could someone be so loved! I didn't deserve it. None of us do.

When we reached the top of the hill, she held on to life for one last breath and then let me know, in her own special way, "I love you. Thank you, but it's my time to go." And then she was gone.

I'm telling you that now so you know how wonderful it was to see her again, full of energy and joy as we ran through the woods in Ruby's trance.

It was as real and as sublime as it was when I was a child. I could smell the pine from the trees. I could feel the brush bounce below my feet. I could see the soft rays of the sun breaking through the trees. A clearing formed ahead and we raced on at full speed. When we reached it, I fell softly into a patch of tall grass and let the sun warm my side. Duchess sat next to me on her haunches, her chest bowed, letting the world know that I was hers. She was my guardian. Then I called her name and she turned into the sweetest, gentlest thing, sniffing her nose against my ear. She licked my face, lay down, and nuzzled against my side. Then, in that warm meadow, we both drifted off into a slumber.

When I awoke from that slumber, I found myself in the midst of a high school baseball game, the trance allowing for easy navigation through time and space. From center field, I could see it all. I saw teammates and childhood friends. Although in a dream, I remembered the moment well and I knew how it would end.

We were a raggedy bunch of players that cared about one thing in the world—winning the game. It was the championship game. During that moment, the meaning of life and our purpose on Earth was further boiled down to one, singular objective—getting one more out.

With two outs and a runner on second, a base hit would tie the game. If they hit a home run, we would lose. I played shallow, close to the infield, betting that I could rob them of a base hit.

Michael—our pitcher, our ace—looked back at the runner on second. This was all just a formality. Michael was in his zone. He was throwing heat and painting the edges of the plate. Michael focused on the batter. We all focused on the batter. Nothing else mattered.

There were two strikes. One more and we win. We had full confidence in Michael. And we had his back too. I took two steps forward, still playing shallow. Michael raised his leg from the stretch, preparing to deliver the final pitch.

Looking back on that moment from the view of decades later in a dream, I still felt goosebumps, even though I knew how it would end. Time slowed almost to a halt, the same way it did when we played the game so many years ago. That's what happens when you enter the zone. Everything slows down, allowing you to focus every ounce of energy on what you must do in that moment. Your mind concentrates on a single mission, drawing from years of instinct, experience, and training.

As Michael delivered the final pitch, we were all dialed in. We were all in the zone.

Center field was my domain. I had earned the position through hard work, a bit of luck, and the gift of raw speed. But mostly because of luck and the help of an unsuspecting bird.

The incident with the bird occurred halfway through the season, months before the championship game on an otherwise uneventful day. Michael and I were standing in center field, comfortably bored and shagging fly balls. It was one of those easy, peaceful days when no one expects anything unusual to happen.

Then, about thirty feet to my side, a small bird landed. Michael saw it first. He nudged my shoulder and pointed to the bird. "Hey, Mel, I bet you can't catch that bird."

No kid worth his salt shies from such a challenge. Of course, I couldn't catch the bird. That would defy the laws of physics. But we kids didn't abide by such laws. And mere physics couldn't discharge me of my solemn duty to catch that bird.

For some unknown reason, the entire team looked toward us almost exactly after the moment when Michael quietly challenged me to catch the bird. At that point, I had no choice in the matter. The bird must become mine. I looked at Michael and smiled. Before he could respond, I burst toward the bird in a flash of speed. Startled, the bird immediately took off in the air. As I raced toward it, everything slowed down. I had entered my zone. The bird zigged right and left while the world around me stood still.

All slowed down so much that I had time to hear my grandfather's words. My grandfather, Papa, had told me many times, "If you can put salt on a bird's tail, then you can catch it." When he threw a football to me, he'd say, "If it hits your fingers, then you should catch it." When I was a kid, I believed everything Papa said.

    I wonder what it must have looked like to the others. I wonder if it looked like but an instant. Surely, no more than a second. Maybe two. Or was it an explosion of dust? From my eyes, I saw the bird's every move. And I moved with it as it zigged and zagged. Right before the bird rose out of my reach, I lunged toward it with all the energy I had to give.

    I hit the ground and rolled across the dusty outfield as one might do after being tossed from the back of a pickup truck. When the cloud of dust settled, I lay on the ground with my hands clasped. Michael came over. He leaned over and said, "No way. There's no way you caught that bird."

    The rest of the team started moving toward us. A few broke out into a jog. With my hands still clasped, I looked up at Michael and smiled. Then I heard it. Just a little tweet at first. As I moved my thumb, the little bird poked its head out. Tweet.

    "Holy bleeping bleep!" Michael said. I stood up and the others stopped in their tracks, their jaws nearly hitting the ground. My coach walked over, wondering what all of it was about.

    "What the hell is going on out here! Boys get back to your . . ." Then he saw me open my hands and toss the bird into the air. It flew away with all its speed.

    Our coach looked up and then at me. "Well, I'll be damned."

    From that point on, center field was mine.

But all of that would mean nothing if the batter hit one over my head in that final, championship game.

    When the pitch left Michael's hand, it raced toward the batter as lightning might race to the ground. And yet, there was a slowness to it too. Because we were all in the zone.

Even the batter was in the zone. The runners were in the zone. Everyone was in the zone.

Some say that the ball left a large dent in the batter's bat. Others say that Michael's pitch was clocked at over 100 miles per hour. I don't know. Several facts remain unconfirmed. But I know this: When the batter hit Michael's pitch, we all knew it was over.

I must have sensed the outcome before the bat made contact. I really don't know. It was as if I'd visualized what would happen next. In that fraction of a second before the batter clobbered the ball, I somehow knew that the ball would clear the fence.

With all of my speed, I raced toward the fence. I didn't look back, not even when I heard the crack of the bat. It all seemed to happen at once. I didn't look back as the ball sailed into the sky. I didn't look back as our entire team put their hands behind their heads. Some fell to their knees, knowing that it had all been lost. I didn't look back as I converged on where I sensed the ball might land. I didn't look back until the split second before I jumped up the fence, placing one foot on it for one final lift, my glove stretched over the fence. The impact was almost as loud as the hit. I fell back onto the field. Everyone stopped. Even the batter stopped. No one knew exactly what had happened. I wasn't sure either. My free hand was clasped tightly over the glove. Then I opened my glove and saw it. As I pulled the ball from my glove and held it up for all to see, the crowd roared and my teammates raced toward deep center field.

It was a simple thing. A little white ball and a small group of boys with no other purpose in life but to play a game. But for a moment, in our small lives, everything in the universe was right.

While in Ruby's trance, I began to understand what she was trying to show me. I began to feel again what it was like to be in the zone.

Then, from high above, as I continued to dream in Ruby's trance, thunder rolled across a dark sky. The childhood game disappeared as quickly as it had arrived. In less than an instant, I was with Duchess again, waking from our slumber in the meadow. She licked my face and I jumped to my feet. Thunder roared again. Lightning hit the ground beside us, setting the grass on fire.

This was not a memory. It was something else. This was something more than a nightmare. As lightning struck again and again, we raced across the field to the edge of the forest.

Dashing about the trees, we fled from the storm as fast as we could. Duchess, though faster, never left my side. I ran in fear, knowing that one misstep would send me stumbling. Duchess feared thunder more than anything else, yet she kept her wits even as lightning cracked all around us. We ran at a superhuman speed. It felt as if we were flying, as if our feet barely touched the ground. Terror flashed everywhere, but we raced forward with laser-like focus. We were in the zone.

While in the trance, I couldn't make sense of it. It all seemed so real, like a memory, but I had never been there before. As Duchess and I raced on, hell seemed to be chasing us. I was running too fast to stop. And I couldn't slow down either. As we raced through the woods, I saw a light shining through the trees as if it were calling us from the other side of the forest. We could make it, I thought. I wanted to get to that light and see what Ruby was trying to show me. As I ran with even greater speed, the light drew closer. It became so bright that it blinded me. The woods began to disappear around us. Then, right before I reached the other side, I heard a deep, dark Shadow laugh. Lightning struck a tree in front of me, turning it into a ball of fire. Running too fast to stop, I lowered my head and jumped into the ball of fire.

Suddenly, I found myself wide awake and dripping sweat. Across from me, I saw Ruby at the table in the dimly lit room of David's church.

Ruby reached toward me gently with her hands. "You've had enough for today. You did well, Mel."

I sat speechless.

Ruby looked at David. "Please, David. Take him home. He'll be ok." Then she turned to me. "It felt good to be in the zone again, didn't it?"

I nodded.

Ruby leaned back and folded her arms, still examining me. "The time will come, Mel, when you must find your zone again. You'll only get one chance and that's only if we're lucky."

She paused and then said, "Mel, you have a gift. You must share it with us. It's not yours to keep."

Her comment startled me. It was exactly what Nero had said the night before.

I squinted my eyes, examining Ruby's expression. *Were Ruby and Nero working together?*

David put his hand on my shoulder. "Let's go, Mel. I'll take you home."

I remained seated, looking directly at Ruby. "No. Not yet."

CHAPTER 15

Dark Forces

"Are you one of them?" I asked, pointing a finger at Ruby. "Are you on their side?"

"Mel," Ruby said. "You have no patience. It's not one of your strengths."

"Lack of patience *is* a strength," I said. "I came here because of Nero's visit. I'm not sure what you're trying to do. Now tell me. Are you on his side? I deserve to know."

Ruby leaned toward me and said, "Yes . . . and no."

"C'mon!" I said, leaning back. "Enough with this cryptic business!"

"Mel, why do you feel the urge to pick sides? Haven't you been listening? Your mind must remain clear during your training."

I said nothing.

Ruby continued calmly, "I suspect that Nero talked about the invisible code."

"Yes."

"The Shadows know it well. Upon their arrival to the other realm, they receive extensive training on the invisible human code. Nero is probably giddy with his newfound knowledge. He wishes he knew the code when he was human like you. I'm guessing that he wants to show you the code. Yes?"

I nodded.

"Are you willing to listen?" Ruby asked.

Again, I nodded and Ruby continued. "Good. We'll start by looking at it from a distance. The invisible code can be whittled down to a single, simple concept. It's this: All humans tend to prefer one way or the other. In everything we do, we feel the urge to pick a specific side. Good or Bad. Right or Wrong. We are programmed to be uncomfortable anywhere in between. That's why you, right now, want to know which side I'm on. You want to know if I am good or if I am evil."

She paused and then said, "Shadows can learn the code in almost an instant. That's because time and space can be bent and shifted in the other realm. Humans need time to understand the code. Humans must be trained."

"You, Mel, have already begun your training on the code. During our first meeting at David's church, I explained one difference between you and David. David acts according to what he *feels* and believes is right. You, well, don't. You analyze the situation and look at it objectively. You weigh the pros and cons of your options. Then you make a decision based on what you *think* is best. You're driven by a desire for the truth. David is driven by a set of values—his set of values."

I interrupted her, "I get that, Ruby. Some people prefer to make decisions based on how they feel while others make decisions based on what they think. So what? Why does this matter?"

"It matters because your ultimate decision—when that moment comes—depends on how well you know the code. And the code is more than just this one tendency of decisions based on feeling or thinking. You must learn many more aspects of the human code. You must understand your own code—your tendencies. You also must know the code of those around you and of strangers too. You must understand why others make decisions and behave in ways you find illogical, selfish, and even reprehensible. To forgive others, you must know their code. To forgive yourself, you must know your code. The time will come when you are asked to make a decision so important that the future of humanity depends on your choice. Without an understanding of the invisible human code and its power over you, you will make a decision consistent with how you are programmed, as if a robot. You, Mel, will make a decision that is reasonable, rational, and what you think is best at the time. That's not a choice. That's how you're programmed. You must learn your code so you know when to depart from it. You must take chances when the odds are against you. You must attempt the impossible. You must choose to take a path few others would take. This ability to choose is what separates the human spirit from all other things. You must embrace it. To do that, you must know your code."

Ruby's energy had reached a new height. She took a deep breath in and then exhaled. Calmly, she said, "Mel, you have so much to learn in such a short amount of time. You must open your mind, take an uncommon leap of faith, and listen to me. You must give me a chance. Will you at least do that?"

I leaned back, folded my arms, and said, "I don't like what's going on. I don't like any of it."

"Naturally," Ruby said.

"I won't promise anything. But I'll listen," I said.

"Good," Ruby said.

"But first," I said. "I have some questions for you."

"Fair," Ruby said.

"Who are the Nephilim?"

Ruby's eyes lit up. "It appears that Nero is in a hurry. We expected that." Then Ruby looked over at David, who had been silent the whole session. "David, show Mel the passages."

David brought over his Bible and opened it to Genesis. David said, "It's an ancient reference in the book of Genesis, one we don't talk about in church. The Nephilim were here when children were born to the sons of God."

"Sons of God?" I asked.

David pointed to the passage in Chapter 6 of Genesis and then read the first four verses to me:

> When people began to multiply on the face of the ground, and daughters were born to them, the *sons of*

God saw that they were fair; and they took wives for themselves of all that they chose. Then the Lord said, "My spirit shall not abide in mortals forever, for they are flesh; their days shall be one hundred twenty years." *The Nephilim* were on earth in those days—and also afterward—when the *sons of God* went in to the daughters of humans, who bore children to them. These were the heroes that were of old, warriors of renown.

David looked up. "A careful examination of the text often leads to surprises. It is something I have become accustomed to. Do you recall us discussing the Nicene Council?"

"Yes."

"Establishing the belief that there is only one son of God and only one God was one of the main purposes of that council. We can only imagine what that debate looked like. Look here, Mel." He pointed to a passage in Chapter 3, a more familiar verse, which read:

> Then the Lord God said, "See, the man has become like one of *us*, knowing good and evil; and now, he might reach out his hand and take also from the tree of life, and eat, and live forever."

David said, "You see where it reads 'man has become like one of *us*'?"

"Yes."

"Now, look at the first chapter of Genesis. Here," he said pointing to verse 26, which read:

> Then God said, "Let *us* make humankind in *our* image, according to *our* likeness; and let them have dominion over the fish of the sea, and over the birds of the air, and over the cattle, and over all the wild animals of

the earth, and over every creeping thing that creeps upon the earth."

David said, "Most readers glaze over those words. They don't pause to wonder what the author meant when he wrote, 'Let *us* make humankind in *our* image, according to *our* likeness'."

"Isn't that a reference to angels or something?" I asked.

David closed the book. "Perhaps. Maybe Ruby can help here. I am still studying these passages and trying to make sense of them. I've been working day and night to become familiar with the text. Ruby says we'll need that knowledge when we climb the mountain."

Ruby looked at me carefully. "Mel, knowledge is a double-edged sword. The Shadows wield such a sword. They know what most of us can't see, or choose not to see. To resist the dark forces, you must clear your mind of all the preconceptions that others have taught you. Can you do that? Can you set aside your beliefs and examine the matters with a critical eye and an open mind?"

"Yes," I responded.

"Then let me ask you this. Do you believe in invisible forces? Do you believe that supernatural powers are around us now? Do you believe that a higher power exists? Do you believe that there are beings, if I can use that word, with an intelligence superior to that of humans?"

I settled down in my seat and thought about all that had happened over the past few months. There was no need to answer.

"Are you prepared to see what Nero can see?" She reached out for my hands again. This time, I didn't resist.

I closed my eyes and began to breathe deeply, listening to Ruby's instructions. I could feel the air enter and leave my body. I could hear it flow, back and forth like waves on a beach. Back and forth, the waves of air moved until I drifted off into a meditative state. All turned dark, but I could hear Ruby's voice.

"Feel the darkness," she said. "It surrounds you. It's always there, trying to suffocate the light within you. Feel its pressure. Sense its presence. Feel the powerful, dark forces at work in our world."

I nodded.

"Good," Ruby said. "Like all forces in the other realm, dark forces are invisible. Yet, they are as real and as constant as gravity. You can't escape them. You know some by name. Doubt. Fear. And Hate. Doubt will stop you in your tracks. It will crush your dreams. It whispers, 'You're not good enough. You're not smart enough. You will lose.' As you work toward what you know you were meant to do, Doubt pushes back with an opposite but greater force.

"Alongside Doubt, Shadows march under the banner Fear. Fear and Doubt want you to fail. That's what they want you to believe—that you will fail. They cloak reason with excuses, prudence with hesitation. They are powerful, convincing forces. They tell you to wait. They tell you that now is not the time.

"Wash away those forces and think of the things you could have done had you followed your heart. Think of the people who have passed from your life, never knowing how much you loved them. Don't let the Shadows blanket those memories with time. Time is not on your side.

"Mel, within you there is a power untapped. It's calling you now. You must listen to the voice inside of you. The one you knew as a child. Once upon a time, it guided you with confidence. It cut through Doubt and Fear with ease. But age has hardened your mind and your heart, quieting the voice. For our mission to prevail, you must listen to that voice. You must let it come to life again.

"Doubt and Fear have oppressed you for far too long. You must push back against them and march toward your destiny."

Ruby paused and I felt the waves of air again. I felt an energy I hadn't felt in a long time. But I felt a darkness too. The darkness weighed on me with a heaviness I had not previously known.

Ruby continued, "The dark forces know you are coming. They are gathering. They'll be waiting for you when you reach the mountain.

"Doubt and Fear are powerful forces. But there is one that plagues us all. It is the one we deny. Ignorance. Humans are not given the knowledge of the Shadows. Ignorance is more insidious than any virus. More lasting than Fear. More destructive than any weapon known to man. None of us are immune. And it leads to Hate. Nothing delights the dark forces more than fostering widespread hate and division. They want us to turn against each other. That is their aim.

"Hate knows no boundaries. It plagues the entire world with Fear and Prejudice, infecting with ease. It delights when we look down on others. It dances when we pick sides. Hate, Fear, and Prejudice unify the ranks. Fueled by the human need to belong, we march in unison toward our own destruction. It turns the North against the South and the East against the West. It turns the Black against the White and the Left against the Right.

"Yes, the dark forces are everywhere. Soon, you will see the dark forces in all of their glory. You will see how easily they can divide and conquer even the purest of souls. You'll witness them tear friends and family apart. The Shadows believe that their time has arrived. They now possess tools with unprecedented reach and power. And it was us humans that built it for them. The Shadows' power has reached an inflection point. They can poison minds with the click of a button and watch it spread like wildfire. Mel, to resist the power of the dark forces, you must learn the invisible code that guides you.

"Mel, soon you will come face-to-face with the dark forces. This is your destiny. It's a burden that you now carry. It's a burden borne by all of us Keepers. We have passed it along to one another for almost two thousand years. The heaviness that you feel is your burden. It will get heavier as you approach the mountain. It will try to crush you as you climb. But you must climb the mountain, Mel. The world now needs to know what has been kept hidden from the dark forces."

As I held Ruby's hands, I could feel her breathing as if we were one. With my eyes closed, I could see the mountain standing before me. I could see the path winding up through the trees and over jagged rocks. I could see the grassy hill looking toward the giant crater. Smoke billowed as if the mountain were breathing. And, as if the mountain were alive, I felt it calling me. I could hear its call. I felt drawn to the peak. Then, I saw myself at the bottom of the trail looking up. David was beside me. I took one step forward and BOOM! The mountain thundered and shook beneath my feet. I heard the sound of Shadows shrieking and howling in the woods. Then, a dark silhouette appeared before me, its head down. Thousands of ranks of Shadows kneeled at its flanks. Somehow, in that moment, I knew before me stood the Dark One. It took one step toward me and I opened my eyes.

Suddenly awake from the trance, I shook and shivered in my chair. Sweat dripped down my face. I looked at Ruby and she asked, "Are you willing to answer the call?"

CHAPTER 16

An Inquiry

"You've made a mistake," I said. "You've chosen the wrong person."

Ruby folded her arms. "I didn't choose anyone. And you don't know what you say. The life you once knew is behind you. You're still here, but it's gone. Tell me, Mel, what more do you need to see?"

Surprisingly calm, I sighed. "Ruby, I'm sorry. But I think you have the wrong person. I'm not built for this."

Ruby stood up from her chair, her voice rising almost to an angry pitch. "Then tell me who is built for this! Why not you? Haven't you been listening? Doubt has infected your brain. You think you're not good enough. You think you'll fail. If failure is your destiny, then quit now."

I lifted my hands in an effort to calm her. "Ok. Ok. Look, I'll listen, but put yourself in my shoes. This is a lot to absorb."

Ruby sat down and looked directly at me with a firmness I had not yet seen. "I have been in your shoes."

Her remark hit hard. I had been so focused on my own woes that I thought little of others, certainly not of Ruby's struggles or her past or the circumstances that brought her to this point. As a mixture of pity, concern, and sincere curiosity welled up within, I said, "I will listen. But first, tell me Ruby, how did you become a Keeper?"

"It was a long, long time ago," Ruby said. "Longer than I expect you to believe. It's enough to say that there was more than gold on the ship we found in the marsh. Yes, I knew of the shipwreck, long before my dear Jesse discovered it. Long before Jesse was alive. It was me who told him where it was. I saw it sink, back when I was a young woman."

"I thought it was a Spanish ship. A galleon," I said.

"It was," Ruby said. "The ship escaped the great storm of 1715. I saw it come in with the tide, only to sink into a deep hole in the river. The box I showed you floated to shore where I stood watching. Mel, it found me."

"1715," I said. "But . . ."

"Yes." Ruby paused, looking deep into my eyes. "Don't you wonder why your health has improved?"

I sat back, a bit startled.

"A Keeper experiences unusual longevity, their life bound to their duty. But this longevity comes with a price, a price that gets heavier with time."

She paused again so I could process what she was telling me. "Mel, I too once had a loving family. A mother. A father. A husband, precious children, and others I loved with all my heart."

My heart sank as she said these words. Aside from Ruby's relationship with Jesse, I assumed that Ruby was mostly a loner. Her reputation as a witch didn't exactly bring her a lot of friends. Jesse was my dad's age and had been Dad's childhood friend. They had fished and explored the marsh off the coast of Georgia. Part of me didn't want to know any more about Ruby. But another part of me needed to know.

"In 1715, I was a slave, but I found happiness with the ones I loved. But one by one, they all left this world. Longevity, Mel, is a curse. Can you imagine what I've witnessed? Can you imagine the burden I've carried? I wouldn't wish it on anyone, not on you and not even on the Dark One himself. But I've carried my burden with dignity and diligence. When my time arrives, I will have done my duty. Mel, this has been the way of the Keepers for centuries. I hope that you are the last one. It must end with you."

She paused again.

"The Shadows will haunt you until your last day, as they have done to all Keepers before you. They want what only you can find. And Shadows will give it to the Nephilim as they bend them to do the will of the Dark One. The Shadows love the Nephilim. They admire their power and influence over others on Earth. But not all Nephilim are dark. Not all are evil. Some still walk the Earth today. I suspect that Nero mentioned some by name."

I nodded, "Yes, he loves Poe. He mentioned Einstein, Beethoven, and Da Vinci. But he seems obsessed with Edgar Allen Poe."

Ruby continued. "Certain people, seemingly ordinary people, can reveal extraordinary things to the rest of us. We call them geniuses or prodigies. We look at their creations with awe and wonder how they did it. We wonder how the human mind could produce such creations. Find one of these special humans who have brought something truly remarkable to this world and ask them how they did it. Ask them where it came from, and then listen. They can't answer those questions, not directly. They don't know where it comes from, but they know it doesn't come from them. Inspiration is not the word. Nephilim can tap into powers that most of us don't understand. The powers—both of light and of darkness—are above us and around us, wanting to share with the world what has already been created. Yes, the Nephilim and their descendants possess great powers, but they are still human. And their power withers over time when they let it wither."

Ruby paused. I looked over at David and then back at Ruby. "Ruby, I'm not one of them. You know that, right?"

Ruby didn't answer. Instead, she said, "Not all of the Nephilim are known. Many go through life undetected by all, including themselves. In this way, they unknowingly keep the line alive. Mel, we all have gifts. But you have an extraordinary gift, one that you and only you can find. You'll have to use that gift when the time comes to face the army of Shadows."

She sighed. "There are certain people in this world who are born with supernatural gifts. Intellect. Strength. Vision. Speed. Even empathy and beauty. All of these things come from the line of the Nephilim. It's in their blood and part of their code, remnants from the legends of old.

"Mel, the burden you bear is real. It will drive you to the mountain. Far more is at stake than your life. Mel, you were chosen for a reason. But if you are to succeed against the dark forces, then you must learn your code and that of others. Without that knowledge, you will fail. The Shadows will stop you in your tracks."

She paused. "Can you open your heart and mind to me and listen?"

I slowly nodded. "Yes."

"Good," Ruby said. "The time has come for you to learn why you think and behave the way you do. We'll start tomorrow."

"Tomorrow?" I asked.

Ruby smiled.

+ + +

Curiosity had taken hold of me. The next morning, I raced to David's church and found Ruby. Without delay, she began, "Let's start with the basics, with what is already known by humans. Mel, are you familiar with Dr. Carl Jung?"

"No," I responded.

"Many years ago, Dr. Jung shared with us fundamental elements of the code. Dr. Jung's code was further developed by the work of two women—Katharine Briggs and her daughter Isabel Briggs Meyers. They remained dedicated to their work even when those around them doubted. Today, millions still study Jung's work and apply it to their lives.

Jung, however, knew far less than even the weakest of Shadows in the dark world. Shadows understand the code with much greater detail. They understand that the invisible code includes an almost infinite number of elements. The code stemming from Dr. Jung's work only has four main elements."

I listened, curious, but a bit confused.

"Let's see if I can describe it in a way *you* can understand. Mel, you understand visual patterns so I'll try to describe it in that way. Visualize a sound wave full of individual section lines. Each section represents a tendency, a preference for one thing or another. A tall line represents a strong tendency toward a certain behavior. A small line represents less of a tendency. The invisible human code, in its simplest form, is like a string of tendencies, like a long sound wave. Dr. Jung's code only had eight lines, based on two tendencies for each of the four elements. Can you see that in your mind?"

I nodded.

"Many people can't. They're not built like you, Mel. Numbers and patterns confuse them. And that's ok. They process information differently, which means you must communicate with those people in different ways."

Ruby looked at David and then continued. "People like David make decisions based on their feelings. David is a Feeler and Feelers make decisions that are consistent with their values. Before making a decision, Feelers think about how the decision will impact them and others."

Then Ruby turned to me. "Mel, you are a Thinker. You make decisions objectively, analyzing the pros and cons of a decision before deciding what is best. Thinkers seek truth and fairness, even if it hurts another person's feelings.

"Feelers seek harmony and affirmation of their beliefs. They like to associate with those who have shared values. Feelers don't like confrontation.

"Thinkers enjoy a good debate. Curiosity, not affirmation, drives the Thinker. Thinkers enjoy playing devil's advocate.

"Feelers are sensitive and can be easily offended, especially when their feelings aren't considered legitimate or of value.

"Thinkers naturally discount the value of feelings, often offending others without even knowing it. Thinkers are thick-skinned, which can be viewed by Feelers as insensitive, distant, and cold.

"Feelers often use people's names in conversation. Those with strong feeling tendencies wear their emotions for all to see. They can appear warm and friendly, and then surprisingly harsh and mean. They can appear sad and crying, and then happy and laughing. One rarely needs to guess how such a Feeler is feeling.

"Thinkers prefer to keep their feelings to themselves.

"In times of conflict, Thinkers see Feelers as too emotional and irrational. Feelers see Thinkers as uncaring. Thinkers see Feelers as fake. Feelers see Thinkers as rude.

"When they don't understand the code, they see the other as wrong. They see the other as selfish. They wonder how the other can behave in such ways. That's because they don't understand each other. They don't understand the code. This provides fertile ground for hate, anger, and division to grow. This is where the Shadows work, preying on those who are unaware."

Ruby paused to let this information sink in, then she continued.

"Mel, these are the very basics, as simple and fundamental as one plus one if this were math. And, until recently, humans have only been equipped with the basics. Now, humans are beginning to understand the code in more detail. In our desire for knowledge and progress, we have built an intelligence that exceeds our own abilities. Data collection has reached a fever pitch, allowing humans to learn the code of others and influence millions with the click of a button. Dark powers use these tools to distort the truth, create fear, and spread hate. This is what the Shadows have been waiting for. Mel, we live in a most dangerous time, the most dangerous time Earth has ever seen."

Ruby paused and then leaned toward me. "Mel, are you familiar with artificial intelligence?"

"No," I responded.

"You should be. It's tracking you now. It knows you better than you know yourself. It knows your code. It can make the rich richer. It can make the powerful more powerful than they've ever imagined. Our intelligence—human intelligence—can't compare. All those before us—Einstein, Beethoven, and Da Vinci—can't compare. The Nephilim—they can't compare. Artificial intelligence learns on its own, increasing its ability at blinding speed. You will soon see what it can do. The tipping point is near. Mel, artificial intelligence is the single greatest threat to humanity."

Ruby stood up and began to pace, which was unusual. After debating what to say next, she found her chair and seemed to calm down. She reached into the box beside her and placed her Bible on the table. "Mel, there are powerful creations in this world that have been shared with the best of intentions. But power tempts all. It can deceive even those with the purest of hearts into believing they are using it for good. The human desire to influence and control is strong. Dark forces prey on this desire. They are masters of twisting words and hearts. They can bend anyone to do their will."

She paused and looked deep into my eyes. Then she pushed her Bible toward me.

"Mel, you must take your training seriously. You must pour your heart and soul into your efforts. You must answer the call that few are able to answer. You must resist the dark forces. They will try to destroy you. They want what you must find. You cannot let them get it. I believe that the lost book is real and that it contains a force and a message that can repel the power of the dark forces. Shadows cannot be allowed to control such things."

I looked at Ruby's Bible on the table. All in the room was still and quiet. Then I seemed to hear a voice inside of me. It was only a whisper at first. Then the voice grew like warm energy rising. Something inside of me was urging me to take hold of Ruby's Bible. Something begged me to give her a chance.

I looked at Ruby. She was nodding, slowly nodding. Could it be that she could hear the voice too? I looked down again at her Bible. My hand reached forward and clasped her book. "So, what do I do now?"

David, who had remained quiet through it all, almost jumped from his chair with excitement. Even Ruby seemed pleased.

"Study it with the most critical eye. Set aside your preconceptions. Analyze the text as if the existence of those you love depends on your understanding of these words," she said. "Memorize the lines and verses. Investigate the origin of these works and ask why they were written. It's a tall order, but you must do it. You'll need that knowledge when you climb the mountain."

I took a deep breath. Part of me didn't want to commit.

"Mel, you are built for this," Ruby responded.

CHAPTER 17

My Studies

There are people in this world who get great satisfaction from completing a task. Their satisfaction grows as they move through their list of things to do. Give this person a stack of papers to go through and they'll methodically go through those papers until they've finished the pile. Then they'll move to the next task and doggedly stay on it until it's done. These people run our companies, our schools, and our community organizations. They're consistently successful at whatever they do. Naturally, I am not one of these people.

People like me leave a trail of unfinished projects behind them. For us to go through a stack of papers, we must believe that the stack of papers matters. We get bored at work if we can't see the value of what we do. It's how we're wired. It's part of our code.

But every now and then we surprise those around us with a near obsessive focus on a task. This can happen for several reasons. If we believe in what we're doing, then we can't let go of the task. We cast aside our natural tendencies and focus on the job until it's done.

We can also achieve the same level of intense focus in times of stress. People who share my code are surprisingly calm and focused in times of extreme crisis. Chaos somehow improves our focus.

Perhaps this is why I became consumed with what Ruby asked me to do. Initially, I resisted. I wasn't immediately interested in studying the text of the Bible. I thought that was an exercise you do to fall asleep. Perhaps you would have felt the same way too. Religion, of all kinds, was on the decline. And it wasn't exactly popular to read the Old and New Testament with a critical eye, searching for inconsistencies and patterns. I wonder now if I would have ever attempted such a task but for the pandemic.

The world was a different place during the year that won't be mentioned. Many of us took on unexpected projects. Analyzing those ancient texts was mine. And it distracted me from a world that was falling apart around me.

My studies began as a mild curiosity, but it didn't take long for me to read things that I'd never heard before. The more I learned, the more I realized I didn't know. When were the letters written? Who actually wrote them and why? Why was the Gospel of John so different from the other three Gospels? Why did Yeshua need to be baptized? Did Yeshua believe that he was the son of God? Who were the Nephilim and the other sons of God? What happens during the afterlife? Do we go there immediately, later, or at all?

Sure, I had heard the opinions of others on some of these issues, but I wanted to know what the text actually said. In little time, I became consumed. I poured my efforts into memorizing the chapters and the verses, trying to learn them by number and order. The numbers and arrangement of the text intrigued me more than anything. Each sentence was like a piece of a giant puzzle, where some pieces fit and some didn't. My mind looked for patterns, putting pieces together in an attempt to see the big picture. That's how I'm wired. It's part of my code. I even began to enjoy the work, every now and then forgetting that a dark cloud hung over the entire world.

Then, in the middle of an otherwise uneventful day, I took a break. Lynn had been bugging me to rake the oak leaves that had fallen. She was the type of person who valued getting things done. She didn't waste time on debating whether raking leaves mattered. And so I raked.

While working in our yard, I heard a deep voice singing. From the corner of my eye, I saw Nero's shadow appear from behind a tree. In a deep voice, he sang:

> Vanity of vanities! All is vanity.
> What do people gain from all the toil
> at which they toil under the sun?
> A generation goes, a generation comes,
> but the earth remains forever.

I immediately recognized the words. It wasn't Poe. Continuing to rake, I said, almost involuntarily, "Ecclesiastes."

Nero smiled. "Yes, the wisdom of Solomon. He's one of my favorites."

I continued to rake. My mind was so full of numbers that I cared little for Nero's presence. In a way, I had almost expected him to come.

Nero walked over to me, watching me rake. "It's all so very pointless, don't you think?"

I kept raking.

Nero looked at the little piles of leaves. "Just let nature happen. Let leaves cover the ground as they were meant to do. Let them decay and provide nutrients for the next generation of trees. How many hours do you waste raking leaves? I bet you cut grass too. You piddle about this property as if it were yours. As if such a thing could belong to a human."

I stopped raking and looked at Nero, "So you came all the way here to haunt me about doing yard work?"

"Oh, come now, Mel. You're far smarter than that. Put down the rake and walk with me."

"No, thanks."

"I hear that your studies are going well," Nero said.

I said nothing.

"Good. It'll help us on the mountain. We'll need your help."

I stopped raking for a moment and asked, "So exactly what do you need me for?"

Nero didn't respond right away. He squinted his eyes and then said, "I have been quite transparent with you, more transparent than your friend Ruby. If you really want to know, us Shadows have our limits too. We must do our work through humans. Through people like you, Mel."

"Good luck with that," I said.

"Stop it," Nero said. "Don't be so arrogant, Mel. You have no idea what we're capable of. You have no idea what influence we have over you and over others too."

I continued my mindless task of raking leaves.

Nero asked, "Has Ruby told you about our science project?"

I glanced sideways at him.

He said, "Artificial intelligence will change the world. Mel, we live in a most interesting time. We are on the brink of something tremendous. We're approaching an inflection point for all of humanity. Soon, humans will no longer be the most intelligent beings. They'll no longer enjoy their position at the top. And here's the beautiful part—it was humans that made all this possible!

"Do you doubt what I say? Look around you, Mel. With unprecedented data, artificial intelligence knows what drives you. AI knows what you want to buy. It knows what you like to read. It knows what attracts you. It knows what disgusts you. It knows what makes you happy. It knows what makes you sad. It knows what makes you angry. It knows what makes you hate.

"Mel, AI knows your code and the code of others. It can turn friends on friends and family on family. It can turn the white on the black and the left on the right.

"Mel, can you see this now? With AI, humans can influence almost anyone, anywhere, at any time. And we Shadows can influence those humans. Mel, nothing can stop us.

"The world is changing, Mel. Those you thought you knew well will surprise you with stunningly selfish behavior. You will witness mass absurdity fueled by mere clicks of a button. All of this is the natural way of humans. It is human nature to want to believe in something. It's human nature to want to belong. And to want to be right. This makes you easy prey. It is a dark and beautiful thing.

"Mel, what you will witness is just the beginning. A much darker era awaits us."

I stood in silence. After all that had happened, I didn't want to believe what I was hearing, but it all made sense. I couldn't respond. Too much of what he said seemed true. As my mind often does, I looked to the future, thinking about my children and the world they would live in. Something must be done. I began to understand what Nero was explaining.

Then the sound of Lynn's minivan pulling into the driveway interrupted my thoughts.

"Ah," Nero said. "She's arrived precisely on schedule."

Lynn got out of the van and was talking on her phone. She walked toward me with a look of concern.

"Yes," she said. "He's right here."

Lynn handed me the phone. "It's your mom. She's been trying to call you."

Putting the phone to my ear, I said, "Mom, what is it?"

"It's your father. He got another scan today. He didn't have a stroke. Son, I don't know how to tell you this. The doctor says it's cancer. I hate to ask you this, but can you come to Camden?"

"Yes, of course."

"Thank you, Son."

CHAPTER 18

Home

As I'm writing this letter to you, I wonder, *How old are you?* You're probably not in your late 30s to mid-40s. Mid-lifers don't have time to read letters. It's a difficult time. I'm not exactly sure why, but I think it has something to do with being completely overwhelmed all the time.

Kids and work are enough. Either one of those alone is enough. Your parents are aging. Some are dying, along with grandparents, aunts, and uncles you hold dear. If you're not in the midst of a divorce (40%), then one of your siblings is or damn near it. If you're not living paycheck to paycheck (70%), then almost everyone around you is. If you're lucky enough to own a house, then it's trying to kill you. In every room, there's stuff everywhere and it sucks up what little time you have to spare. Congratulations, you've made it halfway through life.

If there's one thing that's universal, it's suffering. I'm not sure why, but we all suffer. As Dad suffered, I noticed more and more how others—friends, family, and strangers—also suffered. My family was not unique in that way. But Dad was my father and I loved him with all of my heart. And he loved me. That is natural, I think.

There was something special about Dad. He loved people. He truly loved the people he met in this life, not just his friends and family. He cared about the rich. He cared about the poor. He cared about the black. He cared about the white. He cared about the weak and he cared about the strong. He cared about the left and he cared about the right. Dad radiated an unusual warmth that you felt instantly. And he was the toughest human I have ever known.

Dad was born to serve as the City Manager of Camden, SC. I know this now.

As a kid growing up in Sandy Pines on the outskirts of Camden, the thought never crossed my mind. Or his either, for that matter. Before working for the city, Dad worked at a sawmill. It's been about thirty years since he worked at the mill and Dad hasn't shared this story with anyone but his family. But I don't think he'll mind if I share it now. Hell, in a few hours it'll probably die with me.

Dad had made a living resurrecting failing sawmills. He had spent years helping to turn around a mill near Camden. As was Dad's way, he did this by focusing on taking care of the people who worked there and making sure that all the ranks embraced this approach. In only a few years, the mill became a success. Dad was pleased with what he had helped build and Camden became our home.

The problem with the situation was that the mill was a family business. Dad was not family. The time came to make room for family. Dad was told to fire two supervisors at the mill. These two supervisors happened to be two of the best workers at the mill. They reported directly to Dad. They trusted Dad. They were good men who, like Dad, had established roots in the area.

All of us, I think, face decisions that pull us in two very different directions. We know what the right decision is, but we don't make that decision because it's hard. We quickly rationalize why we should take the easy path, the path we believe is best for us.

Almost thirty years later, I still remember the day Dad came home from work after getting the news. We threw the football in our driveway, for hours it seemed. I was just a kid and Dad didn't say much about what happened, only that something happened at work, that things were going to be ok, but we would need to move to another town.

That's a difficult thing for a kid to understand when all he knows is the little town that he calls home. But we rolled with it, looking at places on a map where we might go. Dad received offers from places all across the States, all from people who knew him and had worked with him before. Before him, lay a promising career.

Camden wouldn't allow him to leave. A friend got him a job as a substitute teacher. When our savings ran out, Dad worked two jobs. Mom taught school. They knew their kids didn't want to leave. So we got by.

After working as a substitute teacher for a few years, he was asked to serve as the finance manager for the local arts center. After helping turn the arts center around, he was asked to serve as the finance manager for the city. It didn't take long for the city to ask him to serve as the city manager. So, in the end, it worked out. It's what some people would call destiny. Serving as the city manager of Camden during the year that won't be mentioned was Dad's destiny. And I guess we owe a bit of thanks to the owners of that old sawmill. Otherwise, he'd still be there and what happened in Camden during the year that won't be mentioned might have turned out differently.

To this day, the two men who kept their jobs at the mill don't know what Dad did for them. And unless they read these letters, they never will. Dad took care of his people. Always. I don't understand why people like my dad must suffer. I don't understand why the Lord takes away from us those who so love the world that they would sacrifice their own well-being for others. These kinds of people have so much good to offer this world. It's not fair. Instead of taking away people like my Dad, the Lord should take people like me.

+ + +

Perhaps, in a few hours or less, I'll get my wish. Darkness set in long ago so it's only fitting that it all ends soon. But I can't let go yet. I must tell you what happened.

I drove home to Sandy Pines as fast as my car would allow. I didn't care if the police stopped me. I didn't care if I hit a bump and sent it all into oblivion. I had left Lynn, the kids, and all my stuff behind. I wanted to go home.

Even under normal circumstances, it's odd to come back home after being gone for way too long. You notice things, changes big and small.

Camden is a small but thriving old town. That's probably unique by itself, but Camden has a touch of history that gives its residents a healthy mixture of pride and identity. There's no doubt the people of Camden love their town and one can't underestimate the importance of this when the town's survival is at stake.

If Camden stands for anything, it stands for courage. Larry Doby, the first black man to play baseball for the American League, hails from Camden. Major General Baron de Kalb, a French military officer who served in the Continental Army, lost his life for our freedom in the Battle of Camden during the Revolutionary War. The Camden area is home to at least four recipients of the Congressional Medal of Honor, with one awarded for actions taken in the past few years. So many examples of great courage from such a small town must be a statistical anomaly, but I'll leave that research to you.

When I crossed the Wateree River, familiar roads welcomed me home. And in a few short minutes, my car stopped in our driveway under a cloud of dust. Inside, I found Dad sitting in his usual chair, relaxed as if everything were going to be ok. Meanwhile, Mom was buzzing around cleaning the room—her form of therapy, I think.

+ + +

Before Dad could stand up straight, I gave him a giant hug. Mom walked over, took a deep breath, and hugged us both.

Perhaps you too have experienced such a moment. Perhaps you have received tough news about someone you loved dearly.

I remember how my throat thickened to where I couldn't speak. None of us spoke. None of us could.

Finally, Mom said, "Breathe, Son. It'll help."

After a few deep exhales, I sat in a chair and asked, "What did the doctor say?"

Dad, now sitting down, leaned forward. "He believes it's brain cancer. The seizure medicine wasn't working, so they did another MRI, this time with contrast. He got us an appointment with a surgeon in two weeks. We'll know more then."

"Could it be something else?" I asked.

Dad shook his head. "The doctor doesn't think so. He's seen this before."

"Dad, I'm so sorry."

"It's ok, Son. It's a lot, but we'll deal with this."

Mom sat down next to me. "Thank you for coming. How's Lynn doing?"

"Good. She's at home with the kids. They're all doing fine."

Mom nodded. "We'll get through this."

I looked at Mom and tried to smile. Mom and Dad didn't deserve such pain. They didn't deserve such suffering. And yet, somehow, they still stayed positive.

I couldn't tell them about what I was dealing with. Enough already weighed on them. I began again to deny my own issues, seeing them as fantastical if not part of a bad dream. Inside, I felt anger boiling. I felt anger because of Dad's situation. I felt anger because of all that was happening. But, at the same time, my parents needed me to help make things better, not worse. They didn't need my anger.

"I'll have radiation following brain surgery," Dad continued. "We're not sure what all of this means, but it sounds like that will last about six weeks."

I nodded, listening.

"Then chemo," Dad said.

"For how long?" I asked.

"We don't know, Son. I'm just sharing what we . . ."

Dad's eye drooped and his body began to seize up. Mom walked over to Dad and put her arm around him. Dad's mouth twitched. It looked as if he was in terrible pain. But Dad stayed steady, as steady as one could be. He couldn't speak. The seizure was too powerful and it kept hold of him for more than a minute.

After it subsided, Mom looked at me. "That's the seventh one today."

I shook my head. "I'm so sorry, Dad. Does it hurt?"

He nodded.

Mom continued, "They've been increasing in frequency. At first, it was only one every few days. Now, it's like this."

"I'm ok," Dad mumbled.

Mom sat down in her chair and Dad stood up. He walked over to the coat rack and put on a blazer, looking as if he were going to work.

"Where are you going?" I asked.

"The office," he said. "If I go now, then I might have an hour or so before the next one hits."

"The office?" I asked, looking at Mom.

"You know your dad."

"I'll be back soon," Dad said. "We'll eat steaks tonight. How does that sound?"

It sounded crazy. That's what I thought. It all sounded crazy.

"Look, Son, I don't know what else to do. The staff needs me. There's a lot going on." Dad picked up his truck keys and opened the door. "Son, I can't just sit here and do nothing.

We're going to fight this thing. We're going to do all that we can, ok?"

I had no response.

"Would you like to come with me?" he asked. "There are people that would love to see you."

I shook my head. "No, thank you. Maybe another time."

"Ok," he said. "I'll pick up some ribeyes for dinner."

+ + +

After Dad left, I walked outside and soon found myself meandering about the woods behind the house. The walk took me to Dad's shed, home to an old lawnmower, a tiller, and several other small engines collecting dust. Half of them worked.

I found a spark plug wrench and began working on one of the broken engines. I cleaned the plug and pulled the cord to crank it but nothing happened. Next, I disassembled and then reassembled the carburetor. It still didn't crank. So I checked the fuel lines for obstructions.

Here's the thing. I don't work on engines. I'm not that mechanically inclined. But in a span of two hours, I had disassembled and reassembled major components on three different small engines.

At some point I paused long enough to think about how I was behaving. It was at that moment when I truly realized that I was on the verge of entering a dark era. I'd been there before after a deployment to Iraq. I know this sounds strange, but people who share my code find themselves, in dark times, fixated on things they would never otherwise do. They withdraw from the life they once knew and behave in ways that are almost completely opposite to their natural tendencies. Because I'd experienced this switch before, I realized what was happening. But I didn't stop. I got lost in the small engines and would have stayed lost in the engines for hours if an unexpected sound hadn't interrupted my work.

A van rolled to a stop in Mom and Dad's driveway. As the side door opened, Tyler and Sophia jumped out. I put the tools down and walked toward home, meeting Lynn as she approached the side door.

"What's going on?" I asked.

Lynn hugged me around the waist. "We want to be here. You're going to need help."

"Thank you," I said.

"How's your dad?" she asked.

"At work."

"What?"

"Yeah. He should be back soon."

Lynn looked at me, noticing the grease on my hands and face, and then sighed. "It's late," she said. "Let's go inside."

COVID was spreading at an exponential rate. Schools had shut down. Most things had shut down, it seemed. "It should last two weeks." That was the line. Some people even believed that.

We were already familiar with the coronavirus before the novel virus spread. A different, more common strain had pushed Tyler's body to the limits several times already.

Soon after we went inside the house, Dad walked in with a pack of ribeye steaks, showing them off with a bit of pride. "A friend from the meat market had these. He brought them out and put them in a cooler in the back of my truck. That's how they're doing business now. He said he doesn't know when he'll get another shipment in."

Tyler and Sophia ran and hugged Dad. Few things could have brought him more joy.

Lynn walked over to Dad and said, "If you don't mind, we're going to stay here for a while."

At that moment, you would have never known that Dad was suffering from brain cancer. He walked around the house full of joy. Full of the basic mobility we all take for granted. It was as if brain surgery, intense radiation, chemotherapy, and all the pain and suffering that follows were an eternity away.

I nudged Lynn to a different room and asked, "Are you sure?"

"Yes," she said.

"We could be here for months," I said.

"I know," she replied.

God, I thought, *she was amazing.* These weren't even her parents. While I'm up at the shed tinkering on useless engines, she's preparing for what needs to be done.

"We'll get through this," she said.

I exhaled a deep, comforting breath. It was as if I'd been holding it in for hours.

I nodded. "Thank you."

Outside, I found Dad at the grill with the ribeyes. He flipped them over the flames with ease, another little thing we took for granted.

"Go get a beer, Son," he said. "Relax."

Dad's steaks sizzled. Mom and Lynn talked in the room near us. The kids played. I sipped on a beer as Dad worked the grill.

We can do this, I thought. *We can get through both the cancer and the crazy pandemic world. Hell, I'd seen worse. I'd spent years deployed with the military overseas.*

Tyler found us outside and climbed into my chair, where we comfortably sat together, watching the fire lick the edges of the steaks.

This time, I thought, *I'd be with my family. This shutdown would be easy. Sure, it would last longer than two weeks. No problem. Social distancing. No problem. The world could use a break from each other. It would be like a deployment. If the world quarantined for a few months, we might learn how to treat the virus. If we worked together, we might form a plan to beat it. People might even emerge from the shutdown grateful for the simple things. The world might emerge a better place, like finding light at the end of a dark tunnel.*

A deep, loud laughter interrupted my thoughts. When I stood up, Tyler almost fell to the ground.

Dad turned to me, "What is it, Son?"

"Did you hear that?" I asked.

"Hear what?"

The laughter boomed even louder.

I looked at Tyler. "Can you hear that?"

"Hear what, Daddy?"

The laughter grew. I walked into the dark woods toward it. I chased the laughter as it moved about the trees. Nothing. Realizing the pointlessness of my pursuit, I walked back home.

"What was it, Son?" Dad asked.

I shook my head. "I'm not sure. I think I'm just tired."

"It's been a long day," Dad said. "Let's eat and then get some rest."

CHAPTER 19

The Battle of Camden

Sleep evaded me that night. I tossed and turned, unable to find any peace. Nero's laughter haunted me. There was enough going on. I didn't need that.

The next morning, I found breakfast on the table. Still in a stupor, I enjoyed a warm plate of grits and eggs. As I took my first sip of coffee, Tyler yelled from the living room. "Daddy, something's wrong!"

In a sprint, I found Tyler looking at the television screen. Someone had left on the news station. Thousands had filled the streets. Few wore masks in a scene of chaos.

Then I saw the headline scroll along the bottom. A white cop had killed a black man and America erupted.

Tyler paced back and forth, turning a Rubik's Cube in his hand. "Daddy, what happened?"

How do you explain all of this to a child? A child who has not yet learned racism. A child who has been told by all those around him to social distance. To quarantine to save people's lives.

A low voice chuckled behind me. I turned and saw Nero's Shadow in my living room almost as clear as if he were there in person. Tyler paced back and forth.

Nero spoke. "Isn't it beautiful what we've done?"

Anger boiled from within as I fought the urge to lunge at Nero. He casually walked over to my side and looked at the screen.

"Amazing, isn't it? Can you now see the power we wield?"

I put my arm around Tyler and said, "Son, give me a hug. I don't know what to tell you right now except a lot of people are really angry."

"But why are they in the streets?"

I knelt down so I could look at Tyler eye-to-eye. "It's their way of expressing their feelings."

"Bullshit," Nero said. "We'll spread that message too. Oh, these are exciting times."

I took a deep breath in.

"Tyler, we'll talk more about this later. I don't yet fully understand what's going on. Can you please go find your mom?"

He nodded and then left the room.

Nero and I both watched the news pan from one crowded street to another. "The Shadows will prevail, Mel. You must accept that. This is just a taste of what is to come."

I sat down on the couch, nearly falling into the seat cushion.

Nero said, "You seem confused. If you knew the code, then all of this would make perfect sense. It's all so very predictable."

Footsteps raced down the stairs. Dad leaned into the living room and said, "I gotta go." Dad looked at the screen full of people in the streets. The news panned to another town, showing people breaking windows and setting buildings on fire. Then Dad looked at me. "We've learned that a group is headed to Camden. People are in the streets now."

Before I could respond, Dad was outside. In a matter of seconds, his truck raced toward City Hall.

"Yes," Nero said, "Camden too will burn."

I put my face in both of my hands.

"Confusion causes stress. I can help you, Mel."

I wanted to ignore him. To forget him. To erase him. But I held no power over Nero or any other Shadows. I watched the screen, trying to make sense of what I saw. For a few minutes, Nero remained silent.

Then he said, "Some of those people feel real pain. Some yearn for fairness. Some want to destroy this country. That matters little; we will use them all. We can bend both the good and the evil to do our will."

Nero leaned toward me and asked, "I can show it to you, Mel. I can show you what Ruby and I have been trying to teach you."

I turned to Nero. "What are you talking about?"

He smiled. "The human code." Then he pointed to my phone. "Pick up your phone, Mel. It's time."

I wanted to resist. I wanted to remain ignorant of Nero's dark ways. But, in an almost involuntary manner, I reached for my phone as if I were under Nero's influence. And yet, a part of me wanted to see the code. A part of me wanted to know.

As I held my phone in the palm of my hand, the screen lit up. He looked at me and smiled. "Never underestimate the power of invisible forces, Mel."

Nero somehow controlled the display, opening programs that showed videos of people on the streets of Camden. "We get to watch it live from the comfort of this living room. Look at them, Mel. Look at their pain and anger."

On the familiar streets of my childhood home, citizens gathered. Some held signs. "I can't breathe." "Justice." "Equality." "United Together."

"It's all so very pitiful, isn't it?" Nero said. "Feelings. Oh, look at all their little feelings pouring out on the streets. They want to be heard. They want to be seen. They want others to see their feelings as legitimate. They want to matter."

The screen turned dark and Nero looked me directly in the eyes. "They don't matter, Mel. You don't matter. None of your little lives matter. You will all die forgotten. Time will erase all memories of your existence. Surely you, Mel, can understand that. You must accept that."

The screen on my phone lit up again. On it, an image appeared in what I can only describe as something resembling a soundwave.

The Life Unlived   121

"This is your code, Mel. Look closer." Nero zoomed in on the soundwave to where I could see a series of individual lines, all of different heights. Thousands of them. Millions of them. They seemed infinite in number.

"Each one of those lines is a tendency, Mel," Nero said. "A preference." He pointed to one tall line. "That one defines beauty. It depicts what you find attractive." He pointed to another line. "That one represents the types of food you enjoy." He kept pointing to lines. "This one identifies where you get your energy from. And this one is your favorite color. This one governs what you like to read. This one captures your favorite songs. There's more to it than these silly tendencies. Look at that section. Here is hate and anger and sadness. That one is fear. These are the valuable ones."

He zoomed in on the lines even more. Each of the lines he had shown me was broken into other lines. They were micro-tendencies, representing preferences within a preference. Details of exactly what I hated and what I feared. Details of what I liked and what I loved. Details of what I valued and what I disregarded. The accuracy of the soundwave blew me away. How could Nero know? Then the screen suddenly turned dark.

I looked at Nero, unable to speak. Nero smiled. "Here's the best part, Mel. Humans created this. Humans with the best of intentions built this for us."

The screen lit up again and showed an image of people in the streets of Camden. Some were shouting. Some were crying. Others were just watching, wondering what would happen next.

"Most of the world is blind to what is happening. Look at them. They're all attached to their phones. Recording almost everything they do. Where they go. What they buy. What they watch. What they like. What they hate. Who they like. Who they hate. They are feeding us an infinite amount of data."

A group of citizens walked down the street arm-in-arm with a sign that said, "United Together."

"Yes, Mel, we're all in it together. That's what makes all of this possible. That and artificial intelligence."

My phone went dark again.

Nero looked into my eyes, this time with no smile. It was a dark, empty, evil look. I felt a hollowness in my soul as he stared at me. "Mel, I know what drives you. I know what you love most. I know what you fear most. You cannot escape our will."

Footsteps approached from the hallway and Tyler walked in, pacing and turning his Rubik's Cube.

Nero smiled.

Anger boiled inside of me like I'd never felt before.

"Easy, killer," Nero said.

The screen on my phone lit up again, showing scenes from the streets of Camden.

Nero nodded at the images. "Feel the anger, Mel. Anger is good. It fuels our fear. And nothing spreads faster than fear."

Suddenly, my phone rang. It was Dad.

"Hey, Dad. What is it?"

"Son, is everyone at the house?"

"Yes."

"Good. Stay there. Things are escalating quickly here. Outsiders have already arrived. People who know nothing about Camden. They've organized a march to City Hall."

"Where are you?"

"City Hall."

"Dammit."

"We'll be ok. Law enforcement is on the way. Hundreds from all over the state. They're staging at the Revolutionary War Center. I've given them orders to stay there. They are not to enter the city limits unless I say so. But if we need them, they're ready. Just stay in the house. I'll be fine."

"Understood."

"Son?"
"Yes?"
"I love you."
"I love you too, Dad."
I put my phone down on the table.
"Oh, isn't that sweet," Nero said, his arms folded. "And very interesting too. No law enforcement in the crowd?"
Tyler paced back and forth, still lost in his cube.
"Tyler," I said. "Come sit with me."
Nero continued, "It's nice to have a father, isn't it? When your time comes, Mel, you'll join me. You will meet the Dark One. That is your destiny. Until then, enjoy this moment of peace."
Peace. That's how Nero described Camden during its darkest hour. And, in hindsight, I understand. None of us saw the unrest coming. None of us knew what would follow. It seemed impossible to predict human behavior.
Racism. How could it still exist? How could it still plague the world? What is it about being human that causes us to hate one another?
Echoes of pain filled the streets. Real pain and cries of why. Then there was the older generation, those who had seen worse. They wanted this to end. This kind of pain belonged in the past. The world and towns like Camden had come so far. This, anyway, is what I had thought, blinded in part by life overseas in the military. Blinded by years spent in a combat zone. Had I forgotten what it was like to live in America?
The march on Camden resurrected feelings and pain that most had wanted to bury. I didn't understand.
"It is quite natural for a human to look down on another human," Nero said, as if reading my mind. "Don't fool yourself, Mel. Don't hold yourself above the monsters who have caused this bit of chaos. Prejudice comes in many wonderful forms. Left versus Right. North versus South.

East versus West. Pick your poison. We Shadows wield it with ease. We can turn nations against nations. States against states. Towns against towns. Neighbors against neighbors. We teach it early. Schools against schools. Teams against teams. Friends against friends. Powered by the human desire to belong and coupled with fear of those they don't understand, prejudice is a very powerful force."

I did not react. I did not respond.

"Do you still doubt the power of invisible forces?" Nero asked. "When will you open your mind and listen to what you know is true? How much pain do you need to see before you submit and accept the truth into your life? Mel, you cannot resist the power of the dark forces. You cannot deny the presence of the Dark One. Set aside your fears and follow me. I can show you the way."

I turned from Nero and squeezed Tyler closer, closing my eyes. God, I wanted the nightmare to end. I wished that life could go back to what it was before. I wished that this was all just a long, bad dream.

When I opened my eyes, I saw the screen on my phone light up again. I picked up the phone. Tyler stood up and began pacing again with his Rubik's Cube. I didn't want Tyler to see what was happening.

The crowd flooded the lawn at the steps of City Hall. Screams and shouts reached a fever pitch. From a bullhorn, someone yelled, "Burn it down! Burn it down! Burn it down!"

I sunk down in a chair and ran my hands through my hair. Tyler paced, working his cube. Nero moved about the room, almost dancing.

I thought about Dad and all his colleagues at City Hall. I could see him sitting at his desk, working the phones and the radio. I could see him moving about the staff, assuring people that they would be ok. They trusted him. But this was out of his control. He knew that. I could see the army of law enforcement staged just outside of town, waiting for their orders. I could see friends from my childhood in the crowd and among the police, both the white and the black. There was an age when such distinctions didn't matter. But no one could ignore reality, the past and the present pain in our streets. I thought about my childhood friends, many of them now fathers like me. How did they—the black, the brown, and the white—explain this to their children? I closed my eyes and tried to see the world from their perspective. It's a very difficult thing to do. Impossible for most of us, if not all of us.

"Burn it down! Burn it down!" rang from my phone.

Tyler paced. I wanted him to leave and to be ignorant of all of this. But what good would that do? He deserved the truth. But I didn't know what the truth was.

"Burn it down!" rang out louder than all of the other chants. On my phone, I saw a young man with a bullhorn race up the steps of City Hall. He turned to the crowd and yelled, "Burn it down!" He threw his fist in the air and shouted again, "Burn it down!" An older black man emerged from the center of the crowd and walked up the steps toward the young man. Then my phone went dark.

Nero stopped. I stopped. Tyler kept pacing. Now at my side, Nero looked at my phone. Nothing. He too seemed confused.

Seconds passed. Nothing. Seconds turned to minutes. Nothing. I tried to call Dad. Nothing. Minutes turned to what seemed like an hour. Nothing. Tyler continued to pace. Nero sat in a corner. I fell back in the chair exhausted. Every bone in my body wanted to race into Camden, go straight to City Hall, race through whatever flames stood in the way, and save Dad. But that was not my place.

Camden was at war, suburban modern warfare at its zenith. It was the closest thing our current population had seen to war. And yet, who was the enemy? It was a force we couldn't see.

The silence reached the point where I could barely stand it. I even stood up to find my car keys. Then, I heard the familiar sound of the side door opening. I found Dad in the kitchen, beaming.

"What happened?" I asked.

"You didn't hear?" he replied. "I'm sorry, I should have called."

Dad described the crowd and the protests exactly as we had seen, a mixture of locals and outsiders marching toward City Hall.

"It was the outsiders who were causing trouble. A young man with a bullhorn was yelling, 'Burn it down!' Some people were asking me to send in the police. We had an army waiting. I couldn't do it. We took a chance on the people of Camden. Then, as the kid with the bullhorn was yelling, 'Burn it down!', a man from Camden, a guy who's lived here all of his life, walked up and took the bullhorn away. He grabbed that kid by the collar, turned the bullhorn in his face, and said, 'Not in my town!' The kid ran away like a scared cat. It was beautiful. Absolutely beautiful."

From the corner of my eye, I saw Nero pacing. That was a first.

"What happened to the crowd?" I asked.

"Some went home. Some are still there."

Tyler had stopped pacing and turning his cube. Dad noticed. "Come over here, Tyler."

Dad gave both of us a big hug. "The people of Camden won today. And their voices were heard. There are very good people in this town. Remember that, Son."

Dad gave us one more squeeze and then ran off to find Mom and the others. Tyler worked his cube again, but this time at a much more casual pace.

I turned to Nero.

He smirked. "So you think you've won something? That good has overcome evil? You think this is over, don't you?"

Nero took a step toward me. "You haven't seen suffering yet. You haven't felt pain. You don't understand the power of the dark forces. This won't last. It never lasts."

I sighed and felt myself smile.

"Mel, you still don't get it. You will submit. You will climb the mountain. You will reveal to the Shadows what the Keystone has kept hidden for far too long."

Keystone? It was the first time I'd heard of a Keystone. Nero immediately sensed my confusion.

"You don't know! She hasn't told you!"

My anger began to boil again.

Nero walked toward me slowly until he was an arm's length from my phone. Nero cut his eyes toward Tyler, who walked back and forth, working his cube.

"Your phone, Mel."

I felt myself lifting the phone toward Nero. When he looked at it, the screen lit up again.

"Would you like to see the Keystone?"

I said nothing.

A small image of a jagged black rock appeared. The screen zoomed in on the rock and I could see little cubed sections on the face of the rock. Nero waved his hand over the Keystone, rotating the sections around its center. There were numbers on the face of each section.

Nero waved his hand over my phone and the Keystone disappeared. Nero smiled and then turned his gaze to Tyler, who was now pacing back and forth again. "Decoding the Keystone requires a very special mind." Then he turned to me. "Mel, you have a gift. It's not yours to keep. You must share it with the world."

Fire suddenly filled my body with rage. I lunged at Nero, reaching for his throat. Passing through his Shadow, I fell to the ground. He laughed a deep, bellowing laugh. Nero seemed to grow in size, his Shadow filling the room with darkness. "You don't know! You really don't know!" he laughed. "And she's hidden it from you all this time."

I stood up from the floor, breathing fast and deep. I would have killed him on the spot if he weren't already dead.

"Anger is good, Mel. Fear is good. They'll drive you up the mountain, that is, if they don't crush you first. Oh, this is exciting! The Dark One must know at once." And in a flash, he was gone.

Tyler, now still and wide-eyed, asked, "What's wrong, Daddy?"

I didn't answer. I had no words. Still full of anger, I walked outside and called David.

"Hello, Mel," David answered.

"Tell Ruby to meet me at the church."

"Mel, where are you?"

"Camden."

"Ok," David said. "When?"

"Now."

CHAPTER 20

The Keystone

I raced down back roads at an incredible speed. A bump in the road might launch my car into the trees, but I didn't care. I cursed Nero. I cursed Ruby. I cursed the whole damned world.

Tyler. He was just a child, unaware of the crazy world that awaited him. He didn't deserve to be a part of this nightmare. He deserved a childhood.

But I couldn't deny his genius. Too busy to give him due attention, I had always seen his gift as a novelty, a curiosity. Others knew more. His teachers noticed more. Those who had perspective noticed more.

As I raced to Savannah, I ruminated over one incident in particular. I couldn't shake it. We were at a school event on Tyler's last day of school when one of his teachers came over to me and Lynn to thank us for letting her teach Tyler. It was an odd sort of thanks because we had no say in who taught Tyler. And if anyone should say thanks, it was us. When Tyler's teacher spoke to us, tears began to fill her eyes.

"I'm sorry," she said. "This isn't like me. I've just never taught someone like Tyler before. And I don't think I ever will."

"What do you mean?" I asked.

Wiping away a tear, she said, "Tyler has a very special mind. And he's so kind to others. Someday, he will change this world. I'm certain of that."

I gave her a confused look.

She motioned us over to her desk. "Let me show you something." Tyler's teacher picked up an object that looked like a jumble of odd-shaped cubes, prisms, and jagged-shaped blocks. She called it a ghost cube, explaining that it had sat on her desk for years as a novelty. You could rearrange the blocks much like you would do with a Rubik's Cube. Of course, nothing ever came of the twists and turns but more jumble. There were no colors or other marks on the faces of the jagged shapes to give you a clue as to how they might fit together. This cube had been in the teacher's family for years, an inheritance of sorts that had been passed down from who knows when. In her mind, it stood for a problem that couldn't be solved.

One day at school, Tyler casually picked the ghost cube up from her desk like someone might pick up a book to read. All the kids were at play so no one noticed, except his teacher. She watched as Tyler looked at the shape, turning it over, noticing things only a mind like Tyler's could notice. Then, with the same casualness, his hands went to work on the cube. He arranged and rearranged the jagged shapes according to patterns and algorithms only known to his mind. All the while, his teacher watched. After a few minutes of turning the shapes over and over, Tyler placed the object down on his teacher's desk. It was in the form of a perfect sphere. Then he walked over to play with his friends.

After sharing this story and a few other similar accounts, Tyler's teacher pleaded with us to challenge his mind and nurture his gifts. But again, I was busy. And at the time, I thought she was just being nice. Sure, Tyler was smart, but a lot of kids are smart. He was just a child and I wanted him to be just a child.

He would not be a part of my nightmare.

Arriving at David's church in record time, I marched into the sanctuary, where I found Ruby waiting at the same table in the same place where all of this began.

Before I reached the table, she stood up.

Looking directly into her eyes, I said, "You lied to me!"

She shook her head. "No."

"You deceived me!"

"It was necessary."

I stopped at the table, my patience paper-thin. "Tell me what you know."

Ruby sighed. "Anger blinds you, Mel. It impairs your judgment. Please, sit down."

"Tyler will not be a part of this. Tell me what you know."

Ruby looked at me, now with a touch of sadness. "Mel, he already is."

I paced back and forth in the dimly lit room, looking for something, anything to throw against the wall.

"Please, Mel. Take a seat. What has happened and what will happen is beyond my control. It is beyond your control. Please, I will share with you all that I know."

"Everything?"

"Everything." It was then when I noticed how Ruby's appearance had changed. She looked older, her hair whiter, her wrinkles more pronounced.

I sat down and asked, "Why didn't you tell me? Why did you keep this from me?"

"You weren't ready, Mel. You would have quit. All would have been lost."

"What makes you think I won't quit now?"

She smiled a gentle smile and extended her hands. For the first time, I could see her veins.

"I don't have much time, Mel," she said. "This will be our last meeting."

When I placed my hands on hers, she gently squeezed them and closed her eyes. "Breathe, Mel. Relax. Feel the air flowing in and out of your body. Breathe."

I was mad, but I closed my eyes and listened to her mantra. Her spell worked quickly and all went dark.

When the darkness cleared, I found myself on Mount Etna, looking at the trail that led through the woods and up the hill that I knew so well. David stood beside me and Tyler was in my arms. I took one step forward and the mountain roared. Lightning flashed and Shadows howled. I fell to my knees, unable to go forward. A deep, dark laughter bellowed from the woods. It was a different laughter than I had heard before. I looked up and saw a dark silhouette approaching. At his flanks, Shadows knelt. I stood up and the dark silhouette laughed again. Lightning flashed and I found myself at the top of the hill. In my hands, I held the Keystone. To one side, I saw the old lava lake, now streaked with fire. Above us darkness swirled. Before me, Shadows knelt as the silhouette walked toward me. I looked down at the Keystone and lightning flashed. I was running for my life as Shadows chased me down the hill, their wailing and howling unbearable. Ash, rocks, and fire fell around us. Then there was a great explosion that sent us tumbling. Lightning flashed and I awoke from the trance.

Ruby opened her eyes and reached into a box, retrieving an odd-shaped object with jagged edges, exactly like the one in my vision. Exactly like the one Nero had shown me on my phone.

Ruby's appearance startled me. She seemed to have aged another thirty years, her hair now white, her body meek and feeble.

In a weary voice, she said, "This is yours now," and pushed the object toward me.

"The Keystone?"

Ruby shook her head. "No. A replica. The real Keystone is on Mount Etna."

The replica felt light in my hands. It seemed to be made of an obsidian-like stone, feeling lighter than glass. I picked up the replica and turned its pieces with ease, as if it were oiled. The craftsmanship was astonishing, for any era.

Ruby continued. "Mel, I have kept this stone for a long, long time. No one has been able to solve it. Not me, nor any of the Keepers before me."

I didn't know how to respond.

"Mel, it's yours now, for you to use as you so choose."

I understood.

"The Keystone will reveal the words of the book that the Keepers have kept hidden for almost two thousand years. Even we don't know what it will say. She pushed the Keepers Codex toward me. You must learn all of these by chapter and verse. There is something in the numbers. The Codex was labeled with numbers for more than just convenience. If you can solve this replica, you can solve the Keystone."

I nodded.

Ruby pulled an envelope from the box. "Inside of this, you'll find a number. Call when you're ready. I've arranged for a pilot to take you to Catania, Sicily, at a moment's notice."

I hesitated, then put the envelope in my pocket.

"Mel, we live in a very small world. You're only half a day away from ending all of this, from doing what you were born to do."

Finally, I spoke. "But what if I can't solve it?"

With sadness in her eyes, Ruby said, "You can't."

I looked to the side. "He's not going with me."

Ruby shook her head. "None of this ends unless the Keystone is solved."

I stood up. "I'll solve it."

"There is courage in you, Mel. You don't lack courage. But you must understand your gifts and the gifts of others. I can't make this choice for you. I have been in your shoes. I do feel your pain, Mel. I too once had a family I loved more than anything in this world."

I sat back down.

"Mel, the dark forces want what we seek. They can't get it. They'll twist its words according to their will. Their power will grow unchecked. You can't let them get the book, Mel. You understand that, right?"

I nodded.

"Good," she said. "Now, what more do you want from me?"

I looked up at Ruby. I wanted to ask her about Tyler, but I couldn't bring myself to mention his name. Yet she knew what weighed on me.

"Mel, if I could carry this burden for you, I would."

Suddenly feeling the weight of what Ruby was trying to say, I felt a lump in my throat and my eyes began to fill with tears. I began to feel Ruby's pain and the pain of others. This was not my way. This was not part of my code. I wouldn't let these feelings sway me from doing what I had already decided to do.

Standing up, I said, "I will solve the Keystone. I alone will do this."

Ruby sighed. This wasn't the first time someone said I couldn't do something. I felt an energy inside of me rising. I began again to feel the anger that had brought me to David's church. I knew what I needed to do.

With the replica in my hand and the envelope in my pocket, I left the church behind me with Ruby sitting at her table. The drive back to my family took a slower pace. The world around me dimmed and I began to slip into a darkness I had known once before. Finding comfort in that familiar transformation, I felt detached from this world as if already dead. For ages, this change has guided men through war, keeping them focused on their mission. And my mission was clear. Solve the Keystone. This was my burden and mine alone.

CHAPTER 21

Darkness

Make no mistake, during the year that won't be mentioned, the world was at war. Darkness and isolation reigned. Everyone suffered. Humanity suffered. Not even the ignorant escaped unscathed.

But we were all ignorant, unaware of how the dark forces played us to do their will. The resurrection of race riots should have clued us in.

How can humanity still harbor such a thing as racism? What can we do to rid this plague from our hearts? Nothing. The disease is as old and as lasting as time. Even if we were to dilute our stereotypes, we would only replace it with some other form of prejudice. As Nero said, it is our way.

Look back at that awful year and you'll see far more than a virus wreaking havoc on our world. Humans seethed with anger and hatred over things like wearing a mask or staying six feet away. Pick a side, any side, and you'll see the other as stupid and wrong. This is our way.

Oh, how the Shadows delighted in the chaos and confusion! It was an election year and politics took on an unusually dark tone. It seemed that a fever had taken hold of the minds of most Americans. And none knew when this fever would break.

Then there was the virus itself, often taking center stage. Many denied it. Some mocked it. And others took absolute refuge in their homes.

Some people simply wanted the truth. They looked for reason and reliable information. They watched the world go mad in stunning fashion, wondering why? How? Even these truth seekers couldn't find what they sought.

Nero was right. Technology had given dark powers the ability to spread misinformation, disinformation, and flat-out lies with the click of a button. Never before had such power been so accessible and so effective.

Yes, the world was at war and, against my wishes, I had been drawn deep into the conflict.

I had been trained for combat, but not for an invisible war. I had been taught things like *"Be polite. Be professional. And have a plan to kill everyone you meet."*

During a gunfight, fire *"Two to the chest. One to the head."*

In combat, *"Hesitation will get you killed."*

When ambushed, *"Run toward gunfire."*

In a physical battle, these guiding principles help one survive. They teach you to see others as either good or bad. They teach you to decide whether another human should live or die. It is a mentality that stealthily rips at one's soul.

Now, tell me, In a war with invisible forces, who is the foe? Who is a friend? My training did not fit invisible warfare.

But some things in war don't change. War means doing without. It means complete focus on the mission. It means simplifying life to survival. War means suffering.

In the year that won't be mentioned, everyone suffered. My family was not unique in that way. It was a world that brought pain and suffering to some of the best of our people. It was a world that preyed on the vulnerable and rewarded the selfish. Few things but death offered an escape from that world, and even that might not prove true.

Hope for a better world seemed to rest on the collective grit of humans. If you're reading these letters from a time far removed from that year and your world turns upside down, then don't expect to find any large quantities of selfless courage from our species. It's not how we are wired, which makes Camden's small victory on the steps of City Hall even more exceptional.

A few days after the crowd dispersed in Camden, Dad underwent brain surgery. The doctors confirmed he had brain cancer, the most aggressive kind. There was no cure. Next, he had prolonged, intense radiation on his brain. Then chemotherapy with no end.

Our family huddled together in Camden. No school for the kids. No friends. No sports. We had been called to care for Dad.

There are some people in this world born to care for others. They can feel another's pain and can comfort them with words and attention. I am not one of these people.

Perhaps you've suffered or cared for a loved one who has suffered from such treatments. Perhaps you understand how the treatments alone can bring a strong human down. If not, then I will spare you from that pain. I wouldn't wish it on even the Dark One himself.

We helped shepherd Dad through the worst of his days, but it was Dad who carried the burden. At six-foot-four and tough as nails, he carried it well. There is a resilience in his generation that most of us don't understand.

He would not let go of his job. And Camden would not let go of Dad. Who does such a thing? A rational person would have resigned and focused on himself, on healing. That's what I would have done. I didn't share Dad's will. I didn't share his love for people.

I hated the world. With each passing day, the world darkened. Even with my rudimentary understanding of the human code, I could see the world for what it was.

We are selfishly made. People do what they want to do. People believe what they want to believe. They seek information they want to be true. They help others because it makes them feel good. Rare is the person who chooses a path of true sacrifice.

All of this brings joy to the dark forces. And we were easy prey. Humans fed information to artificial intelligence at an unprecedented speed and volume, allowing the dark forces to better learn our code. Even humans could target humans based on our code.

As always, as in the days of the Nephilim, we worshiped the strong and the beautiful. But how many of those worshiped ones knew real courage and real sacrifice? Driven by the desire for power and glory, the line of the Nephilim thrived.

Greed abounded. It is what fuels our world. Greed puts people in power. Influence and control are what those in power seek. We worship those who have mastered greed. We worship those who have it all. We worship the strong and the beautiful. We worship those in power when they believe what we want to believe. This is part of our code.

With each day, humanity's stubborn, self-destructive ways increased in speed, accelerating our collective death spiral. People held firm to their opinions and their beliefs, unable to accept facts that proved them wrong. Instead, we twisted and changed facts to fit what we wanted to be true. We insulted those who disagreed.

Hate is a powerful force, able to destroy us deeper than all others. Hate comes in many forms, but darkness always follows.

Yes, the world was engaged in a fierce and real invisible war, where we picked sides, where we aligned values, and where we saw others as friend or foe. Lives were at stake. Souls were at stake. And if one's fate turns on whether they are good or bad, who of us can pass that test? Does any adult alive deserve more than hell?

It was a dark, dark world. And darkness became my home. Do you know it too?

Then you also know that it's not all bad in the darkness. Isolated from the madness of our world, you can find comfort in the peace and quiet of darkness. You realize that it's ok to not belong. You wonder why you ever wanted to belong. There's a clarity that comes with darkness. You see the world for what it is. You see people for who they are. There's no bullshit. No fraud. No fakeness. It's all real. You're not selling anything. You're not trying to get anyone's vote. You need no one's approval. You are real.

In the darkness, I knew that my life didn't matter. I knew that only a few people would miss me when I was gone. When you're already dead, that's ok.

I knew what surrounded me. I knew the only way to escape. I knew that I must solve the Keystone. I alone would face the Shadows. I alone would confront the Dark One. My children and their future children would not have to live in this dark world. The curse must end.

CHAPTER 22

Visions

During moments when I was alone, I tried to solve the replica, moving its pieces according to a seemingly infinite number of patterns and algorithms. None worked. None came close. But I was determined to solve the Keystone.

During breaks from working on the replica of the Keystone, I studied the Codex. I memorized its verses by number, ordering them in my mind. This I could do.

Rare was the time when I found good rest. Sleep didn't come easy. I fought it, as those hours were the best time to work the replica. And when I did find sleep, I didn't find rest. I found more of a half-sleep, where the line between dreams and reality could barely be seen. And in my dreams, visions of the future haunted me.

I wondered if Ruby had also suffered from such visions. I wondered if this was part of being a Keeper.

Of all the visions, five stood out, haunting me more than any others. Here was the first vision:

I'm standing in the midst of a large crowd in a hot, dusty, dirty city. I'm just outside Kabul International Airport, a place I once knew well. Sweat drips down from my dust-covered face. I can feel the heat from the sun bearing down as I look for water.

I'm moving through the thick crowd in an attempt to get to Abbey Gate. Something draws me there.

When I make it to Abbey Gate, I find a group of young Marines standing at their post. They have an impossible job and have approached it in the most unexpected way.

A Marine—a young woman—holds an infant child, rocking it back and forth in an attempt to comfort the crying baby. Another Marine—a young man with a mustache—

playfully douses the hot crowd with cool water from a water bottle. These warriors have brought an uncommon touch of humanity to a dire situation.

When I turn to scan the area, I see Shadows moving about the crowd, whispering to frightened Afghans as they push toward the gate. I can feel the desperation. Yet the Marines stay calm, almost cheerful. They are manning their posts. Behind the host of Shadows, I see him—the Dark One. He remains a distance away, almost just out of sight, his arms folded and his head down, but I know he senses my presence as I sense his.

On the other side of the gate, a jet engine roars to life and a giant military plane moves down the runway. A group of Afghans breach a different gate and chase the plane as it attempts to take off. Shadows dance beside the desperate souls. Some Afghans reach the moving plane, taking hold of any part they can grasp. The crowd watches in horror as the plane takes off, rising hundreds of feet in the air with Afghans still clinging to the plane. As the plane climbs higher and faster, men and women rain down from the plane.

The crowd screams. The Shadows rejoice. Men, women, and children cry. But none run away. There's nowhere to run. They want to be on the next plane.

Hours pass and then tension builds again. You can feel it. You can hear it. You can almost touch it in the air. Shadows move about the crowd even faster than before, whispering and nudging. Always whispering and nudging. Even those who can't see the Shadows know something is about to happen. Something dark is about to transpire. But none run away. There's nowhere to run.

The Marines have been ordered to stand their post. This is their sacred duty.

I stand in awe of their courage. The Marines are so young and full of energy. They have so much to offer this world. When I see them, I can't help but see the friends of my youth.

The pace of the Shadows quickens to a rush. Their whispers rise to a chatter. The chatter escalates to a fever pitch, but no one around seems to notice.

Boom!

The explosion rattles everything around me. For a moment, there's silence. Complete silence. Then a child begins to cry. I'm standing alone in the middle of the blast, surrounded by what is left of the people around me. They're all dead. I fall to my knees and weep, even though I know it's just a dream. The world—the world in my dreams—quickly darkens.

Then there's a bright flash, followed by complete darkness. Ahead of me, a long, dark tunnel forms. In the middle of the tunnel, faces begin to appear. One by one, the faces appear. They are the Marines who had stood their post at Abbey Gate. They're speaking to me. Quietly, at first, then louder. And then I hear them clear and focused. It's a poem. They're reciting a poem in cadence, as if on a march:

> I will take charge of my post.
> In boot camp, that's what they told us to say.
>
> I will take charge of my post.
> But I never thought it would end this way.
>
> I will take charge of my post.
> Over and over, each single day.
>
> I will take charge of my post.
> Began to mean more when deployed far away.
>
> I will take charge of my post.
> But oh how it bores you for hours on end.

I will take charge of my post.
Until that moment you sense the need to defend.

I will take charge of my post.
It all comes so quickly with no time to send.

I will take charge of my post.
Messages to loved ones and childhood friends.

I will take charge of my post.
This is my greatest concern.

I will take charge of my post.
But oh how I wish it weren't my turn!

I will take charge of my post.
Mission first, that's what I've learned.

I will take charge of my post.
My focus is firm.

I will take charge of my post.
That's what you asked me to do.

I will take charge of my post.
In Ramadi, Fallujah, and Benghazi too.

I will take charge of my post.
Others, I will keep safe.

I will take charge of my post.
So you never have to be in my place.

I will take charge of my post.
Here it comes, it's over, the end is near.

I will take charge of my post.
Strange, a peace sets in, I feel no fear.

I will take charge of my post.
It's my time to go.

I will take charge of my post.
There's just one last thing I want you to know.

I will take charge of my . . .

Here was the second vision:

I'm standing in the middle of another large crowd. I see Shadows moving among the people. This crowd is not desperate. They are angry. They are Americans, dressed in ordinary clothes, and moving steadily toward the Capitol.

The crowd begins chanting something that makes the Shadows almost playful in their delight. Behind me, the Dark One watches. Always from a distance, he watches.

As the crowd moves toward the Capitol, they call for the death of the Vice President. Police officers try to steer the mob back. But the crowd is determined. Nothing can hold it back. When they reach the Capitol steps, the Shadows begin to dance.

I stand confused, unable to make any sense of it. And the Dark One watches.

Here was the third vision:

I'm standing in a trench, my feet cold and wet. Beside me, stand men and women armed with rifles and artillery. Explosions rock the ground around us.

The people wear what appears to be make-shift camouflage, as if they put on hunting gear in a rush. I can hear them speaking to one another, but I don't understand the language.

It feels like I am in Eastern Europe during WWII, but it's clearly in the future, almost in the present.

More explosions hit around us and part of the trench caves in. Men and women race to reinforce it with freshly cut timber. I can smell the sap.

I can hear the incoming fire. Right before impact, a man raises his rifle and shouts, "Glory to Ukraine!" The blast sends men and women flying in all directions. Then all goes dark.

Here was the fourth vision:

I'm standing in what feels like a dusty desert. Young men and women are dancing to music. They're happy, almost blissfully so.

Behind them, men on hang gliders quietly descend. Then there's the *pop-pop-pop* of rifles bursting on the crowd. People run and scream as their friends are mowed down by gunfire.

A grenade rolls to my feet and explodes. All goes dark, but only for a moment. When I come to, I find myself surrounded by what appears to be concrete ruins. Men and women are pulling children out of the ruins.

I hear the sound of incoming fire. I look up and see a projectile approaching. *Boom!*

I can't see anything through the fine, gray dust. When it clears, I'm sitting in my living room watching the news. Israel is at war.

Here was the fifth vision:

I'm standing among Naval Officers in the command center onboard the USS George Washington. We watch as, one by one, F-18's launch from the carrier. A map shows that we are somewhere in the South China Sea.

The Commander points to a red dot on the map. It appears to be Taiwan. Other dots move toward the red dot from China. Blue dots move from our location toward the red dot.

On another screen, I see a live feed of what appears to be United States Marines holding a perimeter around an industrial facility. As the camera scans the scene, I see a sign for the building. It's a manufacturing plant for semiconductors. On the map, dots are converging on the red dot.

There is a solemn tone in the room. As the last F-18 departs, none speak. We all know there will be no place to return.

I inhale a deep breath and then close my eyes as I exhale. I know that the vision will soon end.

+ + +

These visions repeat over and over in my dreams during the long, dark months of the year that won't be mentioned. And as I write to you from this bell tower, I thank God that none came true.

CHAPTER 23

A Father's Prayer

If you're still reading these letters, then you must believe in a higher power. You can't believe that we humans are that power. We are weak and selfish and ignorant creatures. Dark forces influence us with ease. We're unable to resist even the most basic forces like fear, doubt, and hate. And if you don't believe in invisible forces, then from where do you think those dark forces flow?

In the year that won't be mentioned, the lines between the days and months blurred. Even now, I recall little more than darkness, confusion, hate, and anger. The power of the dark forces had reached a new zenith and was still climbing.

I hated the world. Let it self-destruct. None of us mattered. All was in vain. You tell me why such a world is worth saving? Why even try?

It was hard to find good in the world. I hadn't always felt this way. As a child, I believed that the world existed in a state of equilibrium, that the bad was in balance with the good. In that awful year, where was the counterbalance? Asleep? Away? Did it exist at all?

Days and months passed—the number I have since forgotten. I tried to solve the replica of the Keystone but failed. The more I tried, the more difficult it seemed. Frustration set in and I began to give up. I began to accept the reality that I couldn't solve the Keystone, not then. Not ever.

Once upon a time, I believed I could do anything. I believed in the impossible. But now I know that's not true. Solving the Keystone was beyond my abilities. I didn't possess such a gift. The only gift I could claim was speed. Raw, useless speed. And that gift too had withered with time.

Finally, in a relatively muted moment, I gave up. Reality sunk in. I placed the replica of the Keystone down on a table in the living room and gave up.

I left the replica behind me and walked down the hall toward a door outside. I needed to take a walk, alone in my defeat. Whatever the Keystone had kept hidden for centuries would stay a secret for ages more.

As I opened the door to go outside, I heard my father call.

"Son, where are you going?" he asked.

I sighed and then looked at Dad, who sat in his usual chair.

"For a walk, Dad," I said. "Just getting some fresh air."

Dad tried to stand from his chair, but couldn't find the strength, the treatment and the disease weighing heavily on him at that moment.

I knew what Dad wanted. He simply wanted me to be with him and visit, a few minutes of my time. He wanted to walk with me.

"Hold on, I'll come with you," Dad said as he tried to get up again but fell back down in his chair.

I closed the door and walked over to a chair near Dad.

As I sat down, he asked, "Son, are you ok?"

Parents know when their children aren't ok.

"I'm ok, Dad."

I'm not the kind of person who asks for help. It's not part of my code. And there's little anyone can do to change that. People who share my code simply get through it. They don't talk their way through a problem. They solve it. Or they exhaust themselves trying.

"Son, there's a lot on your shoulders right now."

I nodded.

"I wish there was something I could do."

"Dad, please. Thank you, but don't worry about me. Look at you," I said.

A long scar ran across the top of Dad's head. His right arm no longer worked. Radiation and chemotherapy had poisoned his body to the edge of its breaking point. Almost unbearable pain gripped portions of his back and his shoulders. And he wanted to know if *I* was ok.

"I'm a mess, aren't I?" Dad said, almost smiling.

"Yeah, Dad. You're a wreck."

"Son, how did we get here?"

"I don't know."

He paused for a moment, then said, "Thank you, Son."

It was a heck of a thing for him to say. To thank me. Who was I to deserve any thanks? That was my first thought. But Dad was sincere. He loved his family and the time we spent with him. He loved his friends. Dad loved people, even those who didn't deserve it.

I walked over and gave him a hug, careful not to cause any more pain to his shoulders.

"You're a good son," he said.

I tried to fight the tears, hugging him a bit longer, hoping he wouldn't notice.

"I'll be back soon, Dad."

"Ok."

"I just need some fresh air," I said, letting go of Dad as I moved toward the door.

Outside, I hurried away from the house. I didn't want any questions or inquiries, just some time alone to process what was happening.

Giving up on the Keystone was easy. But giving up on my family wasn't something I could accept. Yet, now they seemed to be one and the same. The stress blurred my vision and I felt my blood pressure rise. What could I do? It all seemed so out of control.

As I walked around in near blindness, I suddenly felt a warmth on my side, as if the sun had suddenly broken through a patch of clouds.

Then for the first time since that terrifying night across the marsh, I heard her voice.

Rosa.

"It's ok," she said. Then I felt her little hand grip mine. "None of us are perfect."

I fell to my knees and my eyes began to clear.

Warmth filled my heart when I saw her. She smiled and then placed her forehead against mine. She said, "Will you pray with me?"

Though prayer was not my habit, I nodded and closed my eyes. Rosa began to speak. She asked for strength and wisdom. She asked for courage to face what was soon to come. She asked for all of these things on my behalf. Then, in her prayer, she turned to me and said, "Will you come with me?"

"Yes," I said.

A flash like lightning struck and we were taken back in time, back to my home near Savannah on the day of Dad's stroke.

Invisible to everyone, Rosa and I walked beside David and my father in my backyard.

Dad looked at David and said, "I know something is hurting him. I can feel his pain."

David nodded.

Dad said, "You know what's weighing on him, don't you?"

David nodded again.

"But you can't tell me?"

David nodded again.

"Ok," Dad said. "I understand."

Dad and David walked together for a few moments, then Dad said, "Pastor, you don't know me very well and this isn't something I normally ask, but will you pray with me?"

"Of course."

Dad closed his eyes. With David by his side, Dad prayed, "Dear Father, I try not to ask for much and I know you're busy. But I need your help. My son is suffering. I don't know what it is, but I know he's suffering. A father can tell when his child needs help. Please help him, Father. If it's your will, please heal whatever is hurting him. I know my son and he won't tell me what's weighing on him. He doesn't need this burden right now. Please, if it's your will, take away his pain and give it to me. Please, Lord, let me carry it for him."

Before Dad could finish his prayer, he fell to the ground. His right arm began to shake and flail. His right eye drooped. David put his hands under Dad's head to protect and comfort him.

There was another flash and I found myself standing next to Mom. She picked up the phone and dialed a number.

"Hello?" said a voice on the other line.

"Danny, is Mel with you?"

"Yes."

"He needs to come back home now."

There was another flash. I was standing next to Dad and David again. Dad sat up and brushed the leaves off his shirt, looking stunned. Getting his composure back, Dad turned to David. "Please, keep this between us."

David nodded.

There was another flash and I awoke from Rosa's prayer. But she was still beside me. Rosa put her hand on my shoulder and said, "It's time."

I understood. Oh, the burden I had already put on others! My selfish ways must end. I'd been so caught up with my own hate and darkness, I couldn't see.

No more of this Keeper business for thousands of years. The curse must end.

In a soft voice, Rosa said, "It's time for you to go and do what you were called to do."

Almost involuntarily, I nodded.

"The dark forces can be beaten." She touched my heart and said, "The power is inside of you. It's inside of all of us."

I understood.

"You must climb the mountain. You must face the Shadows. You must take a chance on the Keystone and what it holds."

I stood tall and took another deep breath in. "Ok," I said.

"You were chosen for a reason." Then Rosa looked toward my parents' house—my childhood home—and nodded. "Now, go."

Breathing heavily, I walked toward the house. After a few steps, I turned around to say goodbye to Rosa. She waved once more and then faded away as quickly as she had arrived.

When I reached the house, I walked inside and went directly to the living room where I had left the replica of the Keystone. There, Tyler sat on the couch, turning the replica of the Keystone at an amazing speed. In less than a minute, he placed it on the table. It was in the shape of a perfect sphere. I walked over to Tyler and put my arm around him, squeezing him closer. Then I kissed his forehead. It wasn't supposed to end this way.

He picked up the replica and scrambled it. Then he solved it again.

I found my phone and walked into a room where I was alone.

"David?"

"Yes?"

"It's time. Call the pilot and tell him I'm ready to go."

"Are you sure?"

"Yes. I'll call you back again soon, ok?"

"Yes, of course."

Before I could put my phone down, it rang. A Camden number I didn't recognize appeared on the screen. I rarely answer unknown numbers, but I took the call.

It was the mayor and she had the most unexpected request.

CHAPTER 24

Bittersweet

"I need you to get your father to the old ferry crossing this evening," said the mayor. "Can you do that?"

"Yes, ma'am. But why?"

"It's a surprise. Then at dusk, please bring him to the Revolutionary War Center."

"Another surprise?"

"Yes," she said. "Oh, I'm so excited! And a bit nervous too. If he had found out what we were doing, then he would have never allowed any of this to happen."

Getting Dad to the old ferry crossing would be easy. The man loved to ride around Camden and talk about all the projects they were working on.

The environmental park near the old ferry crossing was one of his favorites. It was there, on a bluff on the Wateree River, where traders sailing from Charleston hit rocky shoals and established a trading point to the interior lands. From that old crossing, years before the Revolutionary War, Camden was born.

For me, the river was a place to fish with my dad. We had logged countless, precious hours in a small boat tied off to the branch of a tree hanging over the river's bank. I can still feel the warm sun on my back and see the eddies of muddy water flow past our boat on their way to the ocean. It's such a simple thing, but one I remember clearly even as the end nears.

A few hours before sunset, I told Dad. "I'd like to go for a ride. Do you want to join me?"

He would have jumped out of his chair if he could. Dad's eyes lit up and the plan was put into motion.

"Maybe the kids will want to go with us," I said, walking off to find Lynn. I told Lynn and Mom that the mayor and others had a surprise for Dad. So we all piled into one car and drove toward town.

As we left the neighborhood, I asked Dad, "Where should we go?"

As if he'd been waiting for the question, Dad said, "Let's take the kids to the old ferry crossing. They need to see the environmental park."

"You sure? We could take them to the lake or something," I said.

"No, let's go to the ferry crossing. The gate's closed, but I've got a key."

"Ok," I said.

As we drove to the park, Dad talked about how they had shaped the pond to look like the head of a duck and how they'd built a launch for kayaks and rescue crafts. He talked about the picnic tables, the bird sanctuary, and all the same things I'd heard a thousand times.

When we arrived at the gate, Dad opened his door and said, "I got this."

"I'll help you, Dad."

"No, Son. I can do it."

Somehow, Dad summoned the energy to slowly walk over to the gate with his cane, struggling but determined with each step. He found the lock and fumbled with the key, still learning to use his left hand. I wanted to get out and help, but I resisted.

Finally, the lock fell and Dad pushed the gate open. He walked back to the car, smiled, and said, "Let's go."

We drove down a gravel road, stopping at the ferry crossing. The crossing is a grassy hill that rises to a high point on the bluff. As the sun began to set behind us, I saw what Camden had done for Dad, but he didn't notice. A tingling sensation ran down my spine.

Dad began to slowly walk up the hill, asking Tyler and Sophia to follow. Almost like a tour guide, he talked about the history of the environmental park and the story behind the ferry crossing. I walked over to help Dad climb the hill, but he waved me off. "I got this, Son."

It was hard to watch Dad climb that hill. I couldn't help but think of all the pain and suffering he'd endured. It wasn't fair.

As we approached the top, he noticed a bench positioned so people could watch the river flow by. "That's odd. I don't remember authorizing a bench. I'll have to talk to Public Works about this."

Out of breath and exhausted from the climb, Dad sat on the bench. After catching his breath, he continued talking about the crossing and how the early settlers had sailed up the river until they hit the shoals and then built a ferry crossing to bring trade to the interior. He moved on to the history of Camden until he suddenly stopped.

He saw it. Between him and me, he saw his name on the bench. Then he saw my smile. I pointed to a plaque on the edge of the bluff.

Camden had named the old ferry crossing after him.

I'm not comfortable in emotional moments. It's not part of my code. I didn't know what to say or do so I leaned over and hugged my father.

That special moment, however, was quickly interrupted by my phone ringing. It was the mayor again.

"Well, how did it go?" she asked excitedly.

"Good," I said. "Dad really appreciates what y'all did. Thank you."

"That's a relief," she said. "Some of us thought he might throw the bench into the river. Well, we're all waiting at the Revolutionary War Center. Can you bring him here now?"

"Yes, of course," I said.

As the sun set behind the trees, I began to realize that this was as good as it gets. And I was supremely fortunate to have a father like Dad. He cared about his family and he truly cared about people.

If you've ever wondered if what you do or how you treat people matters, then look at my dad. During a time when national politics turned nasty and people went crazy over COVID, Dad had to make the tough decisions. He did so with grace and with reason, with firmness and with compassion. He didn't let the noise distract him from what he thought was best for the people of Camden. He valued all people, the rich and the poor, the left and the right, the black and the white, and all of those in between. It was this, I think, that made people love him so.

After talking to the mayor, I asked Dad, "Do you feel like going to the Revolutionary War Center?"

"Another surprise?" Dad asked.

"Yes."

He responded, "Isn't the bench enough?"

I nodded, but I explained that people were waiting for him. Friends. Staff. People he had known for decades. He understood. He had to go. And we all knew he wanted to go.

We arrived at the Revolutionary War Center just after dusk. Outside the main building was an old open-air marketplace and courtyard constructed to resemble what it might have looked like about 250 years ago. With lanterns lighting the way, it felt like we had gone back in time.

As I write to you now from this bell tower, the night seems like so long ago. It seems surreal. And yet we were all so happy together in that courtyard a little more than 24 hours ago.

Just yesterday, I was among friends and family in Camden, talking to childhood friends I hadn't seen in over 30 years. And there were others I hadn't seen in almost a year. In my isolation, I had taken those relationships for granted.

For the first time in many months, I saw Danny. It seemed that he'd been away for years.

With two drinks in his hand, he walked over and offered one to me.

"No, thanks," I said.

He nodded. "I was hoping you'd say that." Then he leaned against the wall and sipped on his drinks as we watched the people from our youth trickle in. We both leaned against the wall and watched, saying nothing.

Dad's coworkers were there, too. They were almost giddy with the excitement of getting something past the boss. It didn't take long for Dad to learn that the courtyard at the Revolutionary War Center had been named after him too.

People from all over town arrived. In that courtyard, you could find people from all different walks of life, but they came for the same reason—to honor Dad.

I stayed back and watched, wanting to absorb all that was happening. I almost even forgot that I'd be leaving in just a few hours.

In the middle of the marketplace, Camden had put a piano for the public to play. Midway through the evening, someone began to play a song. As music echoed around the courtyard, a strange thing happened. I began to see, in each person, a glow, like a small candle in the dark. At first, I thought my eyes were deceiving me. But it became clear to me that I could see a real glow in each of them.

Soon after the piano music began, a man began to play a harmonica. As if contagious, the urge to play music spread. A man retrieved a guitar from his car and joined in. Someone else had a flute. The music was unexpected and unplanned. As the impromptu musicians played, people danced and their lights glowed brighter.

I found myself walking among the crowd, drawn to the different glows. As I neared someone's glow, I could feel it. It felt as if I had known the person for all of their life, as if I could sense their gift, as if I could hear a voice inside of them. I could see the fire burning within them. I suppose this was one of Ruby's powers. Perhaps this was part of being a Keeper.

It became clear that every person had a gift, a very special gift. Some were musicians. Some were born to paint. Some were born to teach. Some to coach. Some to heal. Some to care for the sick. Some to build. Some to create. Some to explore. Some to lead. Some to serve.

The call to live the life unlived comes at unexpected times and in unexpected ways. Dad was called to serve as the City Manager of Camden. And he was called to fight brain cancer during one of the world's darkest years.

In my isolation, I had forgotten that humans are amazing creatures. The most amazing of all life on this planet. I could see, in each person in that courtyard, the life they were supposed to live. And yet, in most of them, that life had been dormant, almost asleep. Mine too had remained dormant. What did it take for me to realize that we only have one life and that one life is so very short? Why had I left so much of it unlived? But now I knew what I was called to do.

Surrounded by the glowing lights of the lives unlived, I began to feel anxious, like I was almost late for something. I felt the urge to leave and get the job done. I was ready. Something about that night had changed me. As I looked around the crowd, I realized, perhaps for the first time, all of this was worth saving.

Toward the end of the night, Lynn came over and held my arm. She leaned against me and watched the crowd dance and play in the night. Yes, I thought, this was worth saving.

I felt the urge to look up toward the sky and silently say thank you. For my family. For my friends. For my time on Earth. For everything. I looked up, expecting to see the stars, but instead I saw the words on a sign above the entrance door. It read, "These are the times that try men's souls."

I wondered if the Spirit of the author, Mr. Thomas Paine, was watching us now. I wondered if all the Spirits of the world were watching. Did they know what tomorrow would bring?

Danny caught me looking at the sign. He looked up at it, took a sip from his drink, and said, "That's about right."

Then we leaned back against the building and watched the crowd. It was getting late and I didn't want the night to end, but it was time. I gathered my family and said thank you to all those who had put the ceremony together.

For everyone except me, sleep would come easy. I hadn't told Lynn I was leaving. More than anything, I wanted to tell Lynn. This secret had weighed on me with great heaviness. But if I told her, I would have been too weak to leave, seeing the pain and the confusion in her eyes. How could I tell her such a thing, knowing that I would likely not make it back? And how could I tell her I was taking Tyler with me?

No. I couldn't tell Lynn or anyone else. And this wasn't the first time I'd left her in the middle of the night. Prior military missions required such secrecy and urgency. I'd always hated leaving that way. But, for the first time, I was grateful for those missions. Maybe she would understand.

Exhausted from the night, we put the kids to bed and went to sleep, except I laid down with my eyes wide open. Nothing, not even a trance, could get me to rest. At one point, Sophia woke up.

She had a bad dream and wanted her mommy, so I carried her into our room and placed her in the bed next to Lynn. For hours, I sat beside the bed, writing to Lynn and Sophia. I told them why I had to leave. I told them that I loved them and that I knew they would be strong enough to continue on without us. It wouldn't have been fair to pretend that we would return. I told her, as best I could, about what I had been called to do. I told her where we were going and why. I folded up the letters and put them in a place where only Lynn could find them.

Deep in the night, the hour arrived when it was time to go. I looked at Lynn and Sophia one last time, took a deep breath, and then kissed each of them on the forehead.

CHAPTER 25

Our Flight

I quietly shut our bedroom door and walked over to Tyler's room. Gently placing my hand on his head, I whispered, "Tyler. I need you to wake up, Son."
Barely opening his eyes, Tyler asked. "What time is it?"
"It's early, Son. But we need to go."
"Go? Where?"
"I'll tell you on the way. Please, try not to wake anyone."
Tyler eased out of bed with his eyes still closed. "Ok."
"It'll be a long ride. You might want to bring some books or games."
He slowly nodded.
Holding out a small backpack, I said, "Here, put your things in here. We've got to go now."
Tyler stumbled around the room, feeling his way to a bookshelf. He put a few books in the bag. Then he found one of his Rubik's Cubes and put it in too.
With the bag around my arm, I lifted Tyler up and carried him out of the house as quietly as I could. Outside, the night was clear and I could see the stars above us. A full moon led the way.
"Where are we going?" Tyler asked. "Why is our car parked over there?"
"Shhh," I said. "I'll tell you later."
I put Tyler in the back seat of the car and he fell asleep before we left the neighborhood. Good, I thought. It's better that way.

+ + +

It's interesting how military training kicks in when you need it most. We train and train and train for times of crisis, but rarely does the crisis ever come to be. But when training kicks in, your mind becomes laser-focused on the mission, setting aside all those things that might get in the way.

As we drove to the airport, I went over the plan in my head. If I learned anything about planning in the military, then I learned that the best plan is a simple plan. The other thing I learned was that all plans change. I checked my watch and noted that if all went well, we'd arrive in Catania, Sicily, about two hours before midnight.

Our plan was to fly to the city of Catania, drive up Mount Etna to the hidden trail, retrieve the Keystone, and then run like hell to our rendezvous.

I knew where we were going to meet. I had seen it in several visions. I had seen the lava too, flowing around this bell tower. The visions were always dark and blurry, but I knew the final destination. I just didn't know how it would end. The Shadows would be waiting for us. The odds were against us. The odds were, by any calculation, impossible.

That's what I thought until we arrived at the airport and I saw our pilot.

I nearly ran to hug him. "Sir! So *you're* taking us to Catania!"

"Sorry, Mel," he said. "It's all she could afford. The bird's ready. And please, none of this 'Sir' business. Call me Buckethead." He winked and then continued. "The old lady said, 'No questions. No discussions.' But she told me your name, and that's all I needed to know. Are you ready?"

"Yes."

"Let's do this."

Suddenly, I felt that we had a chance to actually pull this off. Years ago, Buckethead (his call sign) was my boss. He had served as the Commander of Naval Air Station Sigonella in Sicily. Until taking that job, he had flown fighter jets for a living and helicopters for fun. We had a no-kidding Naval Aviator at the stick, someone trained to crash. Like all Navy pilots, he cared little for rules, except the few important ones. This might help us too.

I had served on Buckethead's staff at Sigonella. My job was to provide advice on pretty much any issue that arose. We had worked together on hostage rescues, on operations in Northern Africa, and on "legal" issues with the local governments. There was one issue in particular that mattered now.

A Sicilian town had asked us to use one of our helicopters to lift a statue of Jesus and place it on top of their bell tower. Naturally, I advised Buckethead that this was a bad idea for nearly a thousand reasons. It wasn't part of our mission. We couldn't use U.S. government funds on it. And we're talking about Jesus. What happens when the news media finds out about this?

Buckethead thanked me for the advice and then ordered that we help the locals move the statue. "It's a training mission," he had said. Later, when it was just the two of us, he said, "Mel, you were right and I appreciate your advice. But think about the goodwill we create with the local population. Remember, we are operating from their land. I'll take the fall on this one."

Somehow, Ruby knew. She knew who to pick as our pilot. I looked up, half expecting to see her Spirit. For the first time, I wanted to thank her.

But there was nothing but stars and the hum of the jet engines. I climbed aboard with Tyler in my arms. All the seats were empty except for one.

"You didn't think I'd let you try this alone?" David asked.

"No," I responded. "I expected to see you. Buckethead was the surprise."

David smiled. I eased Tyler into a seat. He hadn't moved much. *Strange*, I thought. I didn't realize it at first, but Tyler was sick. A virus was spreading through his little body. On the plane, I noticed that his breathing rate had increased. I knew the signs. *Shit*, I thought. I'd forgotten to bring his rescue breathing medicine.

Before I sat down, the plane moved forward. Buckethead said nothing over the intercom.

David looked at me and said, "The pilot knows where to go. Ruby gave him strict orders to remain quiet during the entire trip."

David looked at Tyler and noticed his breathing. He didn't say anything, but he understood. Then he turned to me. "So, Mel, what's your plan?"

I explained the simple plan and described the bell tower. "David, your job is to race back down the mountain and ask Buckethead to convince the base Commander to send a helicopter to the bell tower. Buckethead knows the location. If anyone can convince the base Commander to do such a thing, it's Buckethead."

David nodded. We went over the plan several times. On a map, I pointed to the trail, to the bell tower, and to the residence of the base Commander. I knew these places like I knew home. For years in the military, it was my home. We had a chance.

At some point, the hum of the engines lulled me to sleep and I welcomed the much-needed rest. I would need the energy, every ounce I had.

Somewhere over the ocean, turbulence jolted me awake. To my side, I saw David reading his Bible. It was then when I realized that we might actually discover something special. I had been so focused on studying the verses in the Codex and solving the Keystone that I had given little thought to what it might reveal.

I slid into the seat next to David and asked, "David, what do you think we'll find?"

He turned and said, "Mel, I've thought about what we might find every day since Ruby told me about the Keystone." David's voice began to quiver and he fought back tears. "Every single day."

I leaned back, caught off guard by David's sudden emotion.

David regained his composure and said, "Mel, I've spent my entire life searching for answers in this book. For most of my life, I thought it was all there in between the two covers. I didn't stop to think about what might exist beyond this book. I didn't think about what existed before this book was formed. Ever since Ruby told me about the Keystone, I've dreamed of what we might find. Mel, in a few hours, we might see what has been hidden for almost 2,000 years. Think about that."

I nodded, absorbing all that David had to share.

"Mel, ever since I learned the history of the Bible, I've yearned to know what existed before it was created. I know the four Gospels. I'm familiar with Paul's letters. Like you, I can almost recite every page in this book. But I feel like there's something missing. I can almost feel what it is."

He paused, caught his breath, and then continued. "We have letters from Paul. We have a Gospel from Mark, from Matthew, from Luke, and from John. But look at what's not there, Mel."

Like seeing a picture suddenly coming into focus, I realized what David was telling me.

"Mel, imagine what the world would be like if we had a book from *Him*."

My eyes widened and I asked, "Did Ruby mention this?"

David nodded. "All the Keepers believe that is what they have guarded. None of them know. None of them, except for the first Keeper, knew what the Keystone contains."

I thought about the gravity of it all. David continued. "Mel, you know that I was a Jew. Am a Jew."

"Yes," I said.

"So was Yeshua. There was no such thing as Christianity until after Yeshua. And who of us is to say what Christianity means? Who can define such a thing with any authority? Look at what the early writers say Yeshua did and what Yeshua said. He was a revered man. He was and is revered in Islam. His teachings—his ideals—are shared by almost every religion in the world. And yet the world is tearing itself apart as we speak, spoiling Yeshua's name and the message He brought to all those who had no compass to follow. Mel, what if you found a message that could break the feverish madness that has gripped our world?"

David's voice rose. "The dark forces have wielded their power with great effectiveness. They want the Keystone. They want to know what has been kept hidden from them. They want to control it, to twist it, or to destroy it if that is their will."

I had never seen David so fired up. I glanced over at Tyler. Realizing that his tone might wake Tyler, David softened his voice. "Mel, I don't know what you'll find. But I know that you must find it and share it with the world."

David put his hand on my shoulder. "This is what you were called to do." He looked at Tyler, who was still stretched across the seats. "This is what both of you were called to do. It's far bigger than any of us. Far bigger than anything you've ever done. Mel, I wish I could climb that mountain for you. I wish you could give me your burden now. It would be an honor to run up that hill against all of hell.

"But both of us know that I would fail. I don't have the gifts to succeed. You and Tyler were called for a reason and I'll do all I can to help. I will die for you. I will die for Tyler. I will die for this mission. Mel, I do not fear death. And not because I have already died. It is because I am very much alive."

David's words struck hard. I began to feel his passion and his resolve. I felt energy radiating from my soul. I wanted to respond, but I couldn't find the words.

The plane hit turbulence and shook me from the seat. Tyler opened his eyes. I held him and brushed my hand over his eyes, hoping he'd find sleep again. Soon, our plane reached a calm space and Tyler went back to sleep.

In less than two hours, we would land in Catania. With Tyler asleep, I leaned toward David. Without looking up from his Bible, David asked. "What's the first Gospel?"

"Mark," I said, almost involuntarily.

"Good. When was it written?"

"Somewhere between 55 and 60 AD, more than 20 years after Yeshua's death."

"Excellent. Anything written before then?"

"Paul's letters, some of them anyway. We're not sure."

"Right. The next two Gospels after Mark?"

"Matthew and Luke, about the same time, maybe 60 AD."

"And John?"

"Many years later, around 90 AD."

"You'll do well, Mel."

David then quizzed me on the Codex. I almost knew it better than him, my studies in isolation having paid off. We kept this up for over an hour. With about thirty minutes left in the flight, Tyler woke again, the plane shaking and rattling as we flew deeper into a storm. As lightning flashed outside the windows, I looked for something to keep Tyler's attention. David walked around the plane, shutting the window shades. I recognized the storm. I had seen such storms before around Mount Etna as she erupted. The more violent the eruption, the more violent the storm.

Tyler looked at me with the curiosity and surprise that you would expect from a child. "Where are we going, Daddy?"

Home. That's what I wanted to say when he asked. And, in some ways, we were. But I chose my words carefully. "We're going to Sicily, Son. We'll be there soon."

"Sicily?" he asked. "But that's so far away."

"Yes, we've been flying all day. We'll land soon."

The plane shook again and Tyler's eyes opened even wider.

"Daddy, I don't feel well."

"I know, Son. I'm so sorry." I moved next to him and hugged him, holding him tight.

Tyler reached into his bag and found his Rubik's Cube and began shifting its pieces back and forth. It was his way of keeping his mind off the confusion and storm around us.

I handed him the replica of the Keystone. "Here, Son. Work on this one."

Tyler sat his cube aside and began to play with the replica. David and I watched in awe as Tyler's little hands moved the pieces with incredible speed. In less than a minute, Tyler solved it. David looked stunned. I nodded. Tyler scrambled it and then solved it again. He solved it over and over again. Tired of solving it, I suppose, he set the replica aside and asked, "Daddy, will you read to me?"

"Yes, of course."

He reached into his bag and handed me a book. It was a children's book, Tyler's favorite.

Tyler laid down again with his head in my lap. "Read to me, please."

It was a short book, as children's books often are, written in a very simple but beautiful way.

"*The Child Who Wasn't Very Good at Anything,*" I said, then I began to read the story I had read so many times before:

A woman had been told by all of her doctors that she couldn't have children. After years of prayer, she proved them wrong in stunning fashion, giving birth to four children in the same hour. At that moment, the mother dedicated her life to making sure each child lived the best life they could.

Her first was an athlete. He almost sprung out from her womb racing around the room. Her second child was an artist. She could paint pictures with more detail than a photograph. Her third child was a scientist. She absorbed information with ease. No problem was too complicated to solve. Her fourth child was, well, he wasn't very good at anything.

The athlete grew up to be just that—a professional athlete—dazzling everyone in all that he did. Her fourth child, who wasn't very good at anything, worked with all his might alongside his mother to help his brother, the athlete, succeed.

The artist grew up to be just that—a professional artist. She loved her work and all that she had created. All those who saw her work were amazed. As with the athlete, the fourth child, who wasn't very good at anything, worked with all his might alongside his mother to help his sister, the artist, succeed.

The scientist grew up to be a great scientist. She found a life of passion and meaning in her work. As he did with the other two siblings, the fourth child, who wasn't very good at anything, worked with all his might alongside his mother to help his sister, the scientist, succeed.

More than anything, the mother wanted her fourth child to succeed. She wanted him to find his gift and pursue his passion. She wanted him to enjoy life as the other three did.

The fourth child, however, never accomplished much of anything.

Years passed and time brought old age to the mother. She was grateful for her children, and yet, she felt in her heart that something was missing. In her old age, she wanted more than anything for all of her children to be happy.

As her health faded, the mother called all her children home, hoping to see them together one last time. Soon, the family was once again together in their home. She looked at her children, now all grown. She smiled and asked them to come near her for a quiet prayer. In her prayer, she gave thanks and then prayed for happiness for all of her children.

"Oh, Momma," the athlete said. "I can't explain the happiness you have given me. Without you, I would never have made a living from playing a game. If only you could feel the joy I have known."

"Oh, Momma," the artist said. "I can't explain the happiness you have given me. Without you, I would never have made a living from painting. If only you could feel the joy I have known."

"Oh, Momma," the scientist said. "I can't explain the happiness you have given me. Without you, I would never have made a living from studying science. If only you could feel the joy I have known."

The mother beamed with pride as she looked at her children. And yet she couldn't help but think that life wasn't fair. She called her fourth child over, praying in silence that God would give her the right words to share.

But the child who wasn't very good at anything spoke first.

"Mom," he said. "It's hard for me to explain the happiness you have given me, so I wrote it down for you to read." Then he gently placed a folded piece of paper in her hand. He put his arm around his mother, as she read:

> *Dear Mother, I was never very good at sports or school and I can't dance or sing. In fact, when I think about it, I wasn't very good at anything.*
>
> *But through the years, because of you and others too, I have known more happiness than a king.*

She paused and then began to read again,

> *There is an emptiness in one's heart that shows itself when we are alone.*
> *It is the kind of hole, I think, we can never fill on our own.*

She looked up and smiled at everyone in the room.

> *But thanks to you and everyone here, I fill it every day,*
> *   as I watch those I love grow in their own unique and gifted way.*
> *It is my hope and greatest wish of all,*
> *   for everyone to know the joy of helping others when they hear the call.*

With tears in her eyes, she folded the paper and gently placed it in her shirt pocket. Her fourth child, the one who wasn't very good at anything, leaned over and hugged her. "Thank you, Momma, for everything."

+ + +

As I finished the last line of the book, Tyler fell back asleep. He was such a special child. And yet, he didn't know.

CHAPTER 26

The Final Climb

Our brief moment of peace didn't last long. As the plane descended alongside Etna, an incredible storm raged around us. I lifted the window shade up a few inches to see a full moon rising across the night horizon. Above it stood the thick, dark walls of the violent storm. Flashes of lightning lit the way ahead. No rain fell. All the world around us seemed electric and on fire. Etna had already begun to explode. From her main crater, fire shot almost a mile high into the sky. It seemed as if hell were already upon us.

The plane fell fast toward the runway in Catania, landing hard and braking fast. In a near sprint, we ran toward the gates, Tyler still in my arms. With the airport almost empty and no bags to retrieve, we found a rental car in almost no time.

Tyler had become weak and tired, the virus now in full force. After placing him gently in the back seat of the car, I sighed. Perhaps the virus served as a blessing. Had Tyler seen all that raged around him, fear might have seized his mind.

I turned to David and handed him the keys.

David nodded. He understood. As David took the wheel, I sat in the back with Tyler, holding him while he slept, watching his labored breathing as I'd done too many times before.

David drove up the mountain with surprising effectiveness and purpose, navigating an endless number of roundabouts and curvy cobblestone roads. The higher we climbed, the more both Mount Etna and the gathering storm raged, their violence and intensity thickening as we approached a wall of dark clouds.

I cared little for the storm. And hell could wait. David was in the zone. He had been born to shepherd us up that mountain.

As we passed by the bell tower, I pointed, gently tapping the window. David's eyes met mine in the rear-view mirror and he nodded. No words were spoken. I knew that the trailhead would soon appear as the small town disappeared behind us.

When the trail came into view, I pointed and David rolled to a stop. He opened my door and I stood up with Tyler in my arms.

The cold wind cut at my face. Behind it followed an unusually warm gust. Then, as quickly as the mixture of hot and frigid air arrived, a calm descended on the trailhead. The dark clouds gathered together, swirling around Etna's peak.

The stillness of the storm was even more frightening than its violence. It was the quiet that gave me pause. As I looked down at Tyler, doubt crept in. *What had I done?*

Ash began to fall around us while the ground shook. Dark Shadows moved about the trees ahead of us. Staring at the path before us, I said, "We aren't going to make it, are we?"

David said nothing.

I clenched my fist, angry that it would end this way, angry that Tyler was a part of this. This should have been my burden and mine alone.

I told David, "You can't go with me, David. You know that."

Surprising me, David said, "Mel, you can turn back now."

Had doubt taken hold of him too?

Ahead of us, a Shadow howled.

I shook my head. "No. It's time. This must be done."

The Shadows scurried about the trail before us. As I looked up, Etna roared and rumbled. Gritting my teeth, I took one step forward with Tyler still in my arms.

Nausea buckled my knees, bringing me to the ground. I pressed my forehead against Tyler's and fought back tears.

Ahead of me, a Shadow laughed. I recognized his deep, dark laughter. I had heard it in my dreams, felt it in my visions. I knew that the Dark One awaited us on the mountain. His presence, like a blast of wind, almost overwhelmed me. But I looked up, hoping to meet his eyes. I wanted to see his face.

I stood up and took another step forward. Like a pack of hungry wolves, an army of Shadows howled about the trees.

This time, I smiled. I took another step forward. And then another, quickly reaching a jog as the trail met the trees. As I entered the dark forest, I looked back. David was gone.

Deep into the trail, tree branches hit my face as we climbed almost vertically up stone steps. Etna resumed her furious eruptions and lightning cracked so often that it lit the path ahead. A few hundred yards from the top, the trail turned to ash. Our climb was like scaling a cliff in soft sand.

Halfway up the steep mountain ash, I stopped and laid down with Tyler by my side. Exhaustion hit hard and fast. I felt that if I closed my eyes, they would never open again. The ash comforted us like a bed of warm fallen snow. It would have been a peaceful way to go.

But others had given too much for me to stop there. And we had come too far. Energized by the sacrifices of others, I picked Tyler up and made the final climb.

At the end of the trail, we found an unexpected calm. I looked up and saw the eye of the great storm swirling above us. On the edge of the vortex, silhouettes of good and evil gazed upon us as if they had been waiting for us to arrive.

To the North, Etna's great crater billowed and roared. Between us, streaks of red marked the hardened black waves of an ancient sea of lava. To the East, a jagged column of rocks rose toward the sky. To the West, an almost identical column of rocks rose to form a twin peak. It was as if I stood in the center of a horned hill.

Through the eye of the spiraling storm, the moon broke through, shining light on a small grassy field between the two rocky columns. I took a step toward it and Tyler began to stir. After a few steps more, I saw it. The top of the Keystone, almost identical to the one in Tyler's bag, protruded from a hole filled with soft ash. I eased Tyler down and dug around the Keystone with surprising ease. The soft ash fell away like sand. In a few seconds, I held it in my hands.

I pulled Tyler to my chest and whispered, "Son, can you hear me?"

He nodded.

I placed the Keystone in his hands. "I need you to solve this. Can you do that for me?"

He nodded. With his eyes barely open, he began turning the Keystone. He felt its edges with his fingers and turned it some more. He closed his eyes but continued to work the Keystone. Unlike the replica, on each face of the real Keystone was a number. As Tyler turned the faces, I watched the numbers flash by. Tyler kept turning the Keystone in what appeared to me to be a random sequence. He turned it left and right, forwards and backwards, increasing in speed with each turn. The numbers spun about at an incredible speed. His fingers moved even faster. Then, almost in an instant, Tyler made a few quick movements and then handed me the Keystone. It was in the shape of a perfect sphere.

Time stood still as I gazed at it for a moment, afraid to drop it or jumble the numbers. It was a code of some sort. At first, I couldn't make sense of it. But there was a pattern, for sure.

From the rocky hill to our East, drumbeats began, growing louder and louder in a march down the hill. Unfazed, I focused on the Keystone.

I arranged the rounded rows of numbers in my mind, trying to match them somehow with the Codex. As the drums beat louder, my mind worked faster. Realizing that the rows were arranged in sets of three, the answer suddenly came into focus. I knew exactly what I was looking at. It was a beautifully simple code. David was right. We had found the Gospel written in the words of Yeshua.

The beginning of the first three rows read as follows:

1, 5, 3.
1, 5, 4.
1, 5, 5.

Translated, 1 stood for the book of Matthew. 5 for Chapter 5. And 3 for the third verse. Matthew 5:3. It was so simple. The adjacent sets made sense too: 3, 6, 20, and 3, 6, 21. 3 stood for the book of Luke, the third Gospel in the New Testament. 6 for Chapter 6. And 20 for the twentieth verse. Luke 6:20.

I realized that these were verses in Matthew and Luke that weren't found in either Mark or John. In other words, Matthew and Luke were drawing from a source that neither Mark nor John wrote about. The Keystone, like Matthew and Luke, drew from a fifth Gospel—Yeshua's Gospel. Translated, the first verses read like this:

"Blessed are the poor in spirit, for theirs is the kingdom of heaven."

"Blessed are those who mourn, for they will be comforted."

"Blessed are the meek, for they will inherit the earth."

It was more beautiful than I had imagined. And yet, I had read it before. In Matthew. And in Luke too. I felt alive with energy. Laser focused on decoding the rest of the Keystone, I looked at the next set of numbers. But before I could read the next set, I felt a glow behind me, from the hill to our West.

It warmed me so that I turned to face its source. Looking up the hill, I saw them—a host of Spirits radiating with light. They were young and old, many weak and feeble. Around them, I saw the most unexpected congregation of Spirits. Humans, some seemingly frail and disabled, some very young and others very old. There were animals too, some domestic and some wild. There were strangers I'd never met. In the center, I saw the Spirits of friends and family I had once known. My heart stopped when I saw Rosa in the lead.

Smiling, she said, "You've done very well."

Beside her stood Ruby, who also had a face of joy. Behind them were distant family members and childhood friends, many of whom had passed away too soon. But none of the Spirits walked toward me. They stood their ground and waited.

From the East, a horn blew. And the beat of drums echoed around the mountain. I turned to see an army of Shadows standing in formation. They were strong and beautiful, void of blemishes in their darkness. They took the shapes and forms of what we worship and envy. I knew then I was looking at the line of the Nephilim. In the center, stood Nero.

I took one step toward him. Nero flashed an evil smile and raised a horn to his lips. The horn blasted a deafening sound, commanding the Shadows to kneel. All complied except for one. In the silence that followed, the Dark One stood. As the Dark One walked toward me, Nero recited a prayer with the Shadows in chorus.

Do you believe in the Dark One?
Yes, the Shadows said in unison.

Who descended into hell?
Yes.

And rose again to torment those on Earth?
Yes.

He's the one who says you're not good enough?
Yes.

Spreading doubt and fear?
Yes.

You fear him now?
Yes.

Just as you have done before?
Yes.

Because of him, you reject the good?
Yes.

And deny the faith you once knew as a child?
Yes.

He helps you hate others?
Yes.

And seek seclusion from the world?
Yes.

With him, we seek power?
Yes.

And glory?
Yes.

Forever and ever.
Amen.

Then all went silent. While the Shadows knelt, the Dark One continued to march toward me, his head bowed. I stood frozen, nearly paralyzed by the moment.

When the Dark One reached us, he extended his hand with his palm up. I knew what he wanted. I felt a magnetic urge to give him the Keystone.

No, I thought to myself. *Never.*

Then the Dark One looked up and smiled. Stunned, I stumbled backwards.

He was me.

The Shadows howled and jumped to attention, raising their fists and weapons toward the sky. The Dark One laughed. He laughed as I might have laughed. But his laughter was full of evil and darkness.

No. I would never give him the Keystone. I would go to hell before giving up the Keystone.

"As you wish," he said, as if reading my mind. He knew my thoughts. He knew my fears.

He took another step forward. I pulled Tyler to my side and looked back to the host of Spirits. They stood watching, still standing their ground. Both the armies of heaven and hell were waiting on what I did next.

Awake and frightened, Tyler clung to my leg. I wondered if he could see all that I saw. The volcano and the storm alone were enough for nightmares. Could he see the Dark One? And if he saw him, what face did he see?

Tyler's grip tightened. With my eyes now on the Dark One, I handed the Keystone to Tyler. "Scramble it, Son."

Tyler's fingers moved like electricity.

The Dark One roared and then lunged toward us. To our North, Etna erupted and the lake burned with liquid fire. I took the Keystone from Tyler and launched it into the fire.

"You fool!" The Dark One yelled as he rushed to the ledge, where he saw it fall and burn in the red lake below.

When the Dark One turned to unleash his fury on us, we were gone.

Racing down the mountain with all my speed, Etna roared, her crater bursting into streams of fire. Fire lit up the sky as the armies of Shadows and Spirits raced down the horned hills toward one another.

I left all of that behind and didn't look back. I was in the zone. The slopes were too steep for me to run, so I leapt down the ash trail, gliding down the slope as if skiing, jumping rocks as the lava and ash fell around us. Vents burst to our sides, but I didn't care. I was in the zone.

The mountain shook and the battle behind us raged on, but I dared not look back. It was the end of one thing and the beginning of another, a heavenly battle I didn't understand.

Shadows screamed around us from all directions, but I raced down the mountain with Tyler across my shoulders. Energized and still focused on our mission, I bounded down the trail until we found the road and left the alpine grove behind us.

I flew down the black, winding road at a treacherous speed. Rock falls littered the way and a single pebble could have ruined it all, but I was in the zone. I ran as fast as I had ever run, propelled by adrenaline alone. Or was it something else? I don't know. It felt like something else.

From the corner of my eye, I caught a glimpse of a host of Spirits behind me, racing with me. Protecting me. Shielding me from a mass of dark, hissing Shadows. The Dark One led the pursuit. As he edged closer, I felt a pain in my sides. Then my legs went numb. The road around us began to crumble. I knew what he wanted.

But I knew what I had been called to do. I would not let them overcome me.

Suddenly, a wave of brilliance scattered the mass of dark Shadows and I picked up speed. We would make it to the bell tower. I would resist the dark forces to the very end. While in the zone, everything around me disappeared and I focused on what I had been called to do. Space and time no longer mattered. I would do what I had been called to do.

All of hell could have rained down on us and I would not have quit. All the dark forces of the world could have descended upon us, but I would have kept going. Nothing could stop me from reaching the bell tower. Nothing could stop me from writing to you.

CHAPTER 27

The End

We are at the very end now. I have shared with you all that I could. I am now recording what happens as it happens in hopes that these letters somehow transcend time and space, finding a way to reach you, wherever you are.

Tyler is weak, but alive. Etna roars on and I can feel the Shadows approaching. My ears could be deceiving me, but I hear the distant but familiar sound of a helicopter. Could it be? I don't know.

The Shadows must have learned by now that I threw the replica of the Keystone into the fire. We need to get out of here with the real Keystone. There's still more to decode. Perhaps it could help save us from ourselves. But the fire is closing in around us and I fear that it will burn with us.

I am too weak to run and I want to spend my last few moments holding Tyler. Please forgive me if I don't write any more. But I have given you all that I have.

If we don't make it, please tell my family I love them. I am not ready to go, there's so much more to do, but I am at peace.

I wish that Tyler had a chance to live the life unlived–his life unlived. He has so much to offer this world.

The bell tower is shaking now and there's a great roar outside. Either the tower is about to collapse or we are saved.

I can't help but wonder, am I worth being saved? Tyler is, as is every child.

A great light is piercing the bell tower. Could it be? I don't believe it, but it must be true. It's time for us to go. The bell tower will soon fall. If this is truly the end, then I leave you with this—you deserve to live the life unlived. Can you not hear its call? If so, then what are you waiting for? You never know if today will be your . . . .

Acknowledgments

Although this is a work of fiction, many of the places, in particular Mount Etna and Camden, are real. Both are worth visiting. Camden's Revolutionary War Visitor Center is off Exit 98 on Interstate 20 in South Carolina. There you'll find the courtyard and the bench dedicated to my father, Mel Pearson, along with memorials dedicated to Larry Doby, Baron de Kalb, and other heroes of Camden. Pearson Point, also named in honor of my father, rests on a bluff overlooking the Wateree River. It is a short drive away from the Revolutionary War Visitor Center and part of Camden's environmental park.

Invisible, dark forces are real. So is the life unlived. I encourage any artist or writer to read the works of Steven Pressfield. In *The War of Art*, you'll find Mr. Pressfield's take on the life unlived, on invisible forces, and on the source of genius.

You likely recognized Edgar Allan Poe's poem, "The Raven," now in the public domain. Nero made only minor modifications to fit his song.

Lost Gospels have been found and more will be found. I leave that investigation to you, if you're interested.

Official Website (for all books by Jeff Pearson):
www.acrossthemarsh.com

Made in the USA
Monee, IL
14 June 2024